All the Brothers Were Valiant

Ben Ames Williams

Contents

ALL THE BROTHERS WERE VALIANT

VALIANT

BY

Ben Ames Williams

I

The fine old house stood on Jumping Tom Hill, above the town. It had stood there before there was a town, when only a cabin or two fringed the woods below, nearer the shore. The weather boarding had been brought in ships from England, ready sawed; likewise the bricks of the chimney. Indians used to come to the house in the cold of winter, begging shelter. Given blankets, and food, and drink, they slept upon the kitchen floor; and when Joel Shore's great-great-grandfather came down in the morning, he found Indians and blankets gone together. Sometimes the Indians came back with a venison haunch, or a bear steak ... sometimes not at all.

The house had, now, the air of disuse which old New England houses often have. It was in perfect repair; its paint was white, and its shutters hung squarely at the windows. But the grass was uncut in the yard, and the lack of a veranda, and the tight-closed doors and windows, made the house seem lifeless and lacking the savor of human presence. There was a white-painted picket fence around the yard; and a rambler rose draped these pickets. The buds on the rose were bursting into crimson flower.

The house was four-square, plain, and without any ornamentation. It was built about a great, square chimney that was like a spine. There were six flues in this chimney, and a pot atop each flue. These little chimney pots breaking the severe outlines of the house, gave the only suggestion of lightness or frivolity about it. They were like the heads of impish children, peeping over a fence....

Across the front of this house, on the second floor, ran a single, long room like a corridor. Its windows looked down, across the town, to the Harbor. A glass hung in brackets on the wall; there was a hog-yoke in its case upon a little table, and a ship's chronometer, and a compass.... There were charts in a tin tube upon the wall, and one that showed the Harbor and the channel to the sea hung between the middle windows. In the north corner, a harpoon, and two lances, and a boat spade leaned. Their blades were covered with wooden sheaths, painted gray. A fifteen-foot jawbone, cleaned and polished and with every curving tooth in place, hung upon the rear wall and gleamed like old and yellow ivory. The chair at the table was fashioned of whalebone; and on a bracket above the table rested the model of a whaling ship, not more than eighteen inches long, fashioned of sperm ivory and perfect in every detail. Even the tiny harpoons in the boats that hung along the rail were tipped with bits of steel....

The windows of this place were tight closed; nevertheless, the room was filled with the harsh, strong smell of the sea.

Joel Shore sat in the whalebone chair, at the table, reading a book. The book was the Log of the House of Shore. Joel's father had begun it, when Joel and his four brothers were ranging from babyhood through youth.... A full half of the book was filled with entries in old Matthew Shore's small, cramped hand. The last of these entries was very short. It began with a date, and it read:

"Wind began light, from the south. This day came into Harbor the bark **Winona**, after a cruise of three years, two months, and four days. Captain Chase reported that my eldest son, Matthew Shore, was killed by the fluke of a right whale, at Christmas Island. The whale yielded seventy barrels of oil. Matthew Shore was second mate."

And below, upon a single line, like an epitaph, the words:

"'All the brothers were valiant.'"

Two days after, the old man sickened; and three weeks later, he died. He had set great store by big Matt....

Joel, turning the leaves of the Log, and scanning their brief entries, came presently to this--written in the hand of his brother John:

"Wind easterly. This day the **Betty** was reported lost on the Japan grounds, with all hands save the boy and the cook. Noah Shore was third mate. Day ended as it began."

And below, again, that single line:

"'All the brothers were valiant.'"

There followed many pages filled with reports of rich cruises, when ships came home with bursting casks, and the brothers of the House of Shore played the parts of men. The entries were now in the hand of one, now of another; John and Mark and Joel.... Joel read phrases here and there....

"This day the **Martin Wilkes** returned ... two years, eleven months and twenty-two days ... died on the cruise, and first mate John Shore became captain. Day ended as it began."

And, a page or two further on:

"... **Martin Wilkes** ... two years, two months, four days ... tubs on deck filled with oil, for which there was no more room in the casks ... Captain John Shore."

Mark Shore's first entry in the Log stood out from the others; for Mark's hand was bold, and strong, and the letters sprawled blackly along the lines. Furthermore, Mark used the personal pronoun, while the other brothers wrote always in the third person. Mark had written:

"This day, I, Mark Shore, at the age of twenty-seven, was given command of the whaling bark **Nathan Ross**."

Joel read this sentence thrice. There was a bold pride in it, and a strong and reckless note which seemed to bring his brother before his very eyes. Mark had always been so, swift of tongue, and strong, and sure. Joel turned another page, came to where Mark had written:

"This day I returned from my first cruise with full casks in two years, seven months, fifteen days. I found the **Martin Wilkes** in the dock. They report Captain John Shore lost at Vau Vau in an effort to save the ship's boy, who had fallen overboard. The boy was also lost."

And, below, in bold and defiant letters:

"'All the brothers were valiant.'"

There were two more pages of entries, in Mark's hand or in Joel's, before the end. When he came to the fresh page, Joel dipped his pen, and huddled his broad shoulders over the book, and slowly wrote that which had to be written.

"Wind northeast, light," he began, according to the ancient form of the sea, which makes the state of wind and weather of first and foremost import. "Wind northeast, light. This day the **Martin Wilkes** finished a three year cruise. Found in port the **Nathan Ross**. She reports that Captain Mark Shore left the ship when she watered at the Gilbert Islands. He did not return, and could not be found.

They searched three weeks. They encountered hostile islanders. No trace of Mark Shore."

When he had written thus far, he read the record to himself, his lips moving; then he sat for a space with frowning brows, thinking, thinking, wondering if there were a chance....

But in the end he cast the hope aside. If Mark lived, they would have found him, would surely have found him....

And so Joel wrote the ancient line:

"'All the brothers were valiant.'"

And below, as an afterthought, he added: "Joel Shore became first mate of the ***Martin Wilkes*** on her cruise."

He blotted this line, and closed the book, and put it away. Then he went to the windows that looked down upon the Harbor, and stood there for a long time. His face was serene, but his eyes were faintly troubled. He did not see the things that lay outspread below him.

Yet they were worth seeing. The town was old, and it had the fragrance of age about it.

Below Joel, on the hill's slopes, among the trees, stood the square white houses of the town folk. Beyond them, the white spire of the church with its weather vane atop. Joel marked that the wind was still northeast. The vane swung fitfully in the light air. He could see the masts and yards of the ships along the waterfront. The yards of the ***Nathan Ross*** were canted in mournful tribute to his brother. At the pier end beside her, he marked the ranks of casks, brown with sweating oil. Beyond, the smooth water ruffled in the wind, and dark ripple-shadows moved across its surface with each breeze. There were gulls in the air, and on the water. Such stillness lay upon the sleepy town that if his windows had been open, he might have heard the harsh cries of the birds. A man was sculling shoreward from a fishing schooner that lay at anchor off the docks; and a whaleboat crawled like a spider across the harbor toward Fairhaven on the other side.

On a flag staff above a big building near the water, a half-masted flag hung idly in the faintly stirring air. It hung there, he knew, for his brother's sake. He watched it thoughtfully, wondering.... There had been such an abounding insolence of life in big Mark Shore.... It was hard to believe that he was surely dead.

A woman passed along the street below the house, and looked up and saw him at the window. He did not see her. Two boys crawled along the white picket fence, and pricked their fingers as they broke half-open clusters from the rambler without molestation. A gray squirrel, when the boys had gone, came down from an elm across the street and sprinted desperately to the foot of the great oak below the house. When it was safe in the oak's upper branches, it scolded derisively at the imaginary terrors it had escaped. A blue jay, with ruffled feathers--a huge, blue ball in the air--rocketed across from the elm, and established himself near the squirrel, and they swore at each other like coachmen. The squirrel swore from temper and disposition; the jay from malice and derision. The bird seemed to have the better of the argument, for the squirrel suddenly fell silent and departed, his emotions revealing themselves only in the angry flicks of his tail. When he was gone, the jay began to investigate a knot in a limb of the oak. The bird climbed around this knot with slow motions curiously like those of a parrot.

A half-grown boy came up the street and turned in at the gate. Joel remained where he was until the boy manipulated the knocker on the door; then he went down and opened. He knew the boy; Peter How. Peter was thin and freckled and nervous; and he was inclined to stammer. When Joel opened the door, Peter was at first unable to speak. He stood on the step, jerking his chin upward and forward as though his collar irked him. Joel smiled slowly.

"Come in, Peter," he said.

Peter jerked his chin, jerked his whole head furiously. "C--C--C--" he said. "Asa W-W-Worthen wants to s-s-see you."

Asa Worthen was the owner of the **Martin Wilkes**, and of the **Nathan Ross**. Joel nodded gently.

"Thank you, Peter," he told the boy. "I'll get my hat and come."

Peter jerked his head. He seemed to be choking. "He's a-a-a-a-at his office," he blurted.

Joel had found his hat. He closed the door of the house behind him, and he and Peter went down the shady street together.

II

Asa Worthen was a small, lean, strong old man, immensely voluble. He must have been well over sixty years old; and he had grown rich by harvesting the living treasures of the sea. At thirty-four, he owned his first ship. She was old, and cranky, and no more seaworthy than a log; but she earned him more than four hundred thousand dollars, net, before he beached her on the sand below the town. She lay there still, her upper parts strong and well preserved. But her bottom was gone, and she was slowly rotting into the sand.

Asa himself had captained this old craft, until she had served her appointed time; but when she went to the sand flats, he, too, stayed ashore, to watch his ships come in. When they were in harbor, they berthed in his own dock; and from his office at the shoreward end of the pier, he could look down upon their decks, and watch the casks come out, so fat with oil, and the stores go aboard for each cruise. The cries of the men and the wheeling gulls, the rattle of the blocks and gear, and the rich smell of the oil came up to him.... The *Nathan Ross* was loading now; and when Joel climbed the office stairs, he found the old man at the window watching them sling great shooks of staves into her hold, and fidgeting at the lubberliness of the men who did the work.

Asa's office was worth seeing; a strange, huge room, windowed on three sides; against one wall, a whaleboat with all her gear in place; in a corner, the twisted jaw of a sixty-barrel bull, killed in the Seychelles; and Asa Worthen's big desk, with a six-foot model of his old ship atop it, between the forward windows. Beside the desk stood that contrivance known to the whalemen as a "woman's tub"; a cask, sawed chair-fashion, with a cross board for seat, and ropes so rigged that the whole might be easily and safely swung from ship to small boat or back again. Asa had taken his wife along on more than one of his early voyages ... before she died....

At Joel's step, the little man swung awkwardly away from the window, toward the door. Many years ago, a racing whale line had snarled his left leg and whipped away a gout of muscle; and this leg was now shorter than its fellow, so that Asa walked with a pegging limp. He hitched across the big room, and took Joel's arm, and led the young man to the desk.

"Sit down, Joel. Sit down," he said briskly. "I've words to say to you, my son. Sit down." Asa was smoking; and Joel took a twist of leaf from his pocket, and cut three slices, and crumbled them and stuffed them into the bowl of his black pipe. Asa watched the process, and he watched Joel, puffing without comment. There was something furtive in the scrutiny of the young man, but Joel did not mark it. When the pipe was ready, Asa passed across a match, and Joel struck it, and puffed slowly....

Asa began, abruptly, what he had to say. "Joel, the **Nathan Ross** will be ready for sea in five days. She's stout, her timbers are good and her tackle is strong. She's a lucky ship. The oil swims after her across the broad sea, and begs to be taken. She's my pet ship, Joel, as you know; and she's uncommon well fitted. Mark had her. Now I want you to take her."

Joel's calm eyes had met the other's while Asa was speaking; and Asa had shifted to avoid the encounter. But Joel's heart was pounding so, at the words of the older man, that he took no heed. He listened, and he waited thoughtfully until he was sure of what he wished to say. Then he asked quietly:

"Is not James Finch the mate of her? Did he not fetch her home?"

"Aye," said Asa impatiently. "He brought her home--in the top scurry of haste. There was no need of such haste; for he had still casks unfilled, and there was sparm all about him where he lay. He should have filled those last casks. 'Tis in them the profit lies." He shook his head sorrowfully. "No, Jim Finch will not do. He is a good man--under another man. But he has not the spine that stands alone. When Mark Shore was gone ... Jim had no thought but to throw the try works overside and scurry hitherward as though he feared to be out upon the seas alone."

Joel puffed thrice at his pipe. Then: "You said this morning that for three weeks he hunted Mark, up and down the Gilbert Islands."

Asa's little eyes whipped toward Joel, and away again. "Oh, aye," he said harshly. "Three weeks he hunted, when one was plenty. If Mark Shore lived, and wished to find his ship again, he'd have found her in a week. If he were dead ... there was no need of the time wasted."

"Nevertheless," said Joel quietly, "James Finch has my thanks for his search; and I'm no mind to do him a harm, or to step into his shoes."

Asa smiled grimly. "Ye're over considerate," he said. "Jim Finch was your brother's man, and a very loyal one. As long as he is another's man, he is content. But he has no want to be his own master and the master of a ship, and of men. I've askit him."

Joel puffed hard at his pipe; and after a little he asked: "Sir, what think you it was that came to Mark?"

Asa looked at him sharply, then away; and his accustomed volubility fell away from him. He lifted his hands. "Ask James Finch. I've no way to tell," he said curtly.

"Have you no opinion?" Joel insisted.

The ship owner tilted his head, set finger tip to finger tip, assumed the air of one who delivers judgment. "Islanders, 'tis like," he said. "There's a many there." He looked sidewise at Joel, looked away. Joel was nodding.

"Yes, many thereabouts," he agreed. "But there would have been tracks. Were there none?"

"Mark left his boat's crew," said Asa. "Walked away along the shore. That was all."

"No tracks?"

"They saw where he'd left the sand." The ship owner shifted in his chair. "Seems like I'd heard you and Mark wa'n't too good friends, Joel. Your a'mighty worked up."

Joel looked at the little man with bleak eyes. "He was my brother."

"I've heard tell he forgot you was his, sometimes."

Joel paid no heed. "You think it was Islanders?"

Asa kicked the corner of his desk, watching his foot. "What else was there?"

"I've nothing in my mind," said Joel, and shook his head. "But it sticks in me that Mark was no man to die easy. There was a full measure of life in him."

Asa got up awkwardly, waved his hand. "We're off the course, Joel. What about the **Nathan Ross**? Ready for sea, come Tuesday. I'm not one to press her on any man, unwilling. Say your say, man. Do you take her? Or no?"

Joel drew slowly once more upon his pipe. "If I take her," he said, "we'll work the Gilberts first of all, and try once again for a sign of my brother Mark."

Asa jerked his head. "So you pick up any oil that comes your way, I've no objection," he agreed. "Matter of fact, that's the best thing to do. Mark may yet live." His eyes snapped up to the others. "You take her, then?"

Joel nodded slowly. "I take her, sir," he said. "With thanks to you."

Asa banged his hand jubilantly on his desk. "That's done. Now ..."

The two men sat down at Asa's big desk again; and for an hour they were busy with matters that concerned the coming cruise. When a whaleship goes to sea, she goes for a three-year cruise; and save only the items of food and water, she carries with her everything she will need for that whole time, with an ample allowance to spare. She is a department store of the seas; for she works with iron and wood, with steel and bone, with fire and water and rope and sail. All these things she must have, and many more. And the lists of a whaleship's stores are long and long, and take much checking. When they had considered these matters, Asa sent out to the pierhead to summon Jim Finch, and told the man that Joel would have the ship. Joel said to Finch slowly: "I've no mind to fight a grudge aboard my ship, sir. If you blame me for stepping into your shoes, Mr. Worthen will give you another berth."

Finch shook his head. He was a big, laughing man with soft, fat cheeks. "No, sir," he declared. "It's yours, and welcome. Your brother was a man; and you've the look of another, sir."

Joel frowned. He was uncomfortable; he had an angry feeling that Finch was too amiable. But he said no more, and Finch went back to the ship, and Asa and Joel continued with their task.

While they worked, the afternoon sun drifted down the western sky till its level rays were flame lances laid across the harbor. A fishing craft at anchor in mid-stream hoisted her sails with a creak and rattle of blocks and drifted down the channel with the tide. The wheeling gulls dropped, one by one, to the water; or they lurched off to some quiet cove to spend the night. Their harsh cries came less frequently, were less persistent. The wind had swung around, and it was fetching now from the water a cold and salty chill. There was a smell of cooking in the air, and the smoke from the *Nathan Ross*' galley, and the cool smell of the sea mingled with the strong odor of the oil in the casks ranked at the end of the pier.

The sun had touched the horizon when Joel at last rose to go. Asa got up with him, dropped a hand on the young man's shoulder. They passed the contrivance called a "woman's tub"; and Asa, at sight of it, seemed to be minded of something. He stopped, and checked Joel, and with eyes twinkling, pointed to the tub. "Will you be wishful to take that on the cruise, Joel?" he asked, and looked up sidewise at the younger man, and chuckled.

Joel's brown cheeks were covered with slow fire; but his voice was steady enough when he replied. "It's a kind offer, sir," he said. "I know well what store you set by that tub."

"Will you be wanting it?" Asa still insisted.

"I'll see," said Joel quietly. "I will see."

III

The brothers of the House of Shore had been, on the whole, slow to take to themselves wives. Matt had never married, nor Noah, nor Mark. John had a wife for the weeks he was at home before his last cruise; but he did not take her with him on that voyage, and there was no John Shore to carry on the name.

John Shore's widow was called Rachel. She had been Rachel Holt; and her sister's name was Priscilla. Rachel was one of those women who suggest slumbering fires; she was slow of speech, and quiet, and calm.... But John Shore and Mark had both loved her; and when she married John, Mark laughed a hard and reckless laugh that made the woman afraid. John and Mark never spoke, one to another, after that marriage.

Rachel's sister, Priscilla, was a gay and careless child. She was six years younger than Joel, and she had acquired in babyhood the habit of thinking Joel the most wonderful created thing. Their yards adjoined; and she was the baby of her family, and he of his. Thus the big boy and the little girl had always been comrades and allies against the world. Before Joel first went to sea, as ship's boy, the two had decided they would some day be married....

Joel went to supper that night at Priscilla's home. He was alone in his own house; and Mrs. Holt was a person with a mother's heart. Rachel lived at home. She gave Joel quiet welcome at the door, before Priscilla in the kitchen heard his voice and came flying to overwhelm him. She had been making popovers, and there was flour on her fingers--and on Joel's best black coat, when she was done with him. Rachel brushed it off, when Priss had run back to her oven.

They sat down at table. Mrs. Holt at one end, her husband--he was a big man, an old sea captain, and full of yarns as a knitting bag--at the other; and Rachel at one side, facing Priss and Joel. Joel's ship had come in only that day; the **Nathan Ross** had been in port for weeks. So the whole town knew Mark Shore's story. They spoke of it now, and Joel told them what he knew.... Rachel wondered if there was any chance that Mark might still be alive. Her father broke in with a story of Mark's first cruise, when the boy had saved a man's life by his quickness with the hatchet on the racing line. The town was full of such stories; for Mark was one of those men about whom legends arise. And now he was gone....

Priscilla listened to the talk with the wide eyes of youth, awed by the mystery and majesty of tragic things. She remembered Mark as a huge man, like a pagan god, in whose eyes she had been only a thin-legged little girl who made faces through the fence.... After supper, when the others had left them in the parlor together, she said to Joel: "Do you think he's dead?" Her voice was a whisper.

"I aim to know," said Joel.

Rachel looked in at the door. "You needn't bother with the dishes, Priss," she said. "I'll do them."

Priscilla had forgotten all about that task. She ran contritely toward her sister. "Oh, I'm sorry, Rachel. I will, I will do them. Joel and I...."

Rachel laughed softly. "I don't mind them. You two stay here."

Priscilla accepted the offer, in the end; but she had no notion of staying in the tight-windowed parlor, with its harsh carpet on the floor, and its samplers on the walls. She was of the new generation, the generation which discovered that the night is beautiful, and not unhealthy. "Let's go outside," she said to Joel. "There's a moon. We can sit on the bench, under the apple tree...."

They went out, side by side. Joel was not a tall man, but he was inches taller than Priscilla. She was tiny; a dainty, sweetly proportioned creature, built on fine lines that were strangely out of keeping with the stalwart stock from which she sprung. Her hair was darker than Joel's; it was a brown so dark that it was almost black. But her eyes were vividly blue, and her lips were vividly red, and her cheeks were bright.... She slipped her hand through Joel's big arm as they crossed the yard; and when they had found the seat, she drew his arm frankly about her shoulders. "I'm cold," she said, laughing up at him. "You must keep me warm...."

The moon flecked down through the leaves upon her face. There was moon-light on her cheek, and on her mouth; but her thick hair and her eyes were shadowed and mysterious. Joel saw that her lips were smiling.... She drew his head down toward hers.... Joel was flesh and blood; and she panted, and gasped, and pushed him away, and smoothed her hair, and laughed at him. "I love you to be so strong," she whispered, happily.

He had not told them, at supper, of his promotion. He told Priscilla now; and the girl could not sit still beside him. She danced in the path before the seat; she perched on his knee, and caught his big shoulders in her tiny hands and tried to shake him back and forth in her delight. "You don't act a bit excited," she scolded. "You don't act as though you were glad, a bit. Aren't you glad, Joe? Aren't you just so proud?..."

"Yes," he told her. "Of course. Yes. Yes, I am glad, and I am proud."

"Oh," she cried, "I could--I could just hug you in two." She tried it, tightening her arms about his big neck, clinging to him.... He sat stiff and awkward under her caresses, thrilling with a happiness that he did not know how to express. He felt uneasy, half embarrassed. Her ecstasy continued....

Then, abruptly, it passed. She became practical. Still upon his knee, she began to ask questions. When would he sail away? She had heard the *Nathan Ross* was almost ready. When would he come back? When would he be rich, so that they might be married? Would it be long?...

Joel found tongue. "We will be married Monday," he said slowly. "We will go away--on the *Nathan Ross*--together. I do not want to go alone."

She slipped from his knee, stood before him. "Why, Joel! You're--you're just crazy to think of it."

He shook his head. "No," he said. "No, I have thought all about it. It is the best thing to do. We will be married Monday; and we will make a bigger cabin on the--Nathan Ross...." His voice always slowed a little as he spoke the name of his first ship. "You will be happy on her," he said. "You will like it all.... The sea...."

She returned to his knee, tumbling his hair. "You silly! Men don't understand. Why, I couldn't be ready for ever so long. And I wouldn't dare go away with you. For so awfully long. I just couldn't...." Her eyes misted with thought, and she said quite seriously: "Why, Joel, we might find we didn't like each other at all. But we'd be on the ship, with no way to get away from it ... for three years. Don't you see?"

Joel said calmly: "That is not so; because we know about--liking each other, already. I know how it is with you. It is clothes that you are thinking about. Well, you can get them in the stores. And you have many, already. You have new dresses whenever I see you...."

She laughed gayly. "But, Joel, you only see me once in three years. Of course I have new dresses, then. But I just couldn't...."

She laughed again, a faint uneasiness in her laughter. She left his knee, and sat down soberly beside him. She was feeling a little crushed, smothered ... as though she were being pushed back against a wall. Joel said steadily:

"Mr. Worthen will be glad to know you go with me. And every one will be glad for you...."

She burst, abruptly, into tears. She was miserable, she told him. He was making her miserable. She hated to be bullied, and he was trying to bully her. She hated him. She wouldn't marry him. Never. He could go off on his old ship and never come back. That was all. She would not go; and he ought not to ask her to, anyway. To prove how much she hated him, she nestled against his side, and his arm enfolded her.

Joel had not the outward seeming of a wise man; nevertheless he now said:

"The other girls will all be envying you. To be married so quickly, and carried away the very next day...." Her sobs miraculously ceased, and he smiled quietly down upon her dark head against his breast. "Every one will do things for you.... The whole town.... They will come down to see us sail away."

He fell silent, leaving his words for her consideration. She remained very quiet against his side for a long time, breathing very softly. He thought he could almost read her thoughts....

"It will be," he said, "like a story. Like a romance." And the word sounded strangely on his sober lips.

But at the word, the girl sat up quickly, both hands gripping his arm. He could see her eyes dancing in the moonlight.... "Oh, Joe," she cried, "it would really be just loads of fun. And terribly romantic.... Wonderful!" She pressed a hand to her cheek, thinking: "And I could...."

She could, she said, do thus and so....

Joel listened, and he smiled. For he knew that his bride would sail away with him.

IV

In the few days that remained before the **Nathan Ross** was to sail, there was no time for remodeling her cabin to accommodate Priscilla; so that was left for the first weeks of the cruise. There were matters enough, without it, to occupy those last days. Little Priss was caught up like a leaf in the wind; she was whirled this way and that in a pleasant and heart-stirring confusion. And through it all, her laughter rang in the air like the sound of bells. To Joel, Sunday night, she said: "Oh, Joe ... it's been an awful rush. But it's been such fun.... And I never was so happy in my life."

And Joel smiled, and said quietly: "Yes--with happier times to come."

She looked up at him wistfully. "You'll be good to me, won't you, Joel?" He patted her shoulder.

They were married in the big old white church, and every pew was filled. Afterwards they all went down to the piers, where Asa Worthen had spread long tables and loaded them so that they groaned. Alongside lay the **Nathan Ross**, her decks littered with the last confusion of preparation. Joel showed Priscilla the lumber for the cabin alterations, ranked along the rail beneath the boathouse; and she gripped his arm tight with both hands. Afterwards, he took Priscilla up the hill to the great House of Shore. Rachel had prepared their wedding supper there....

At a quarter before ten o'clock the next morning, the **Nathan Ross** went out with the tide. When she had cleared the dock and was fairly in the stream, Joel gave her in charge of Jim Finch; and he and Priscilla stood in the after house, astern, and looked back at the throng upon the pier until the individual figures merged into a black mass, pepper-and-salted with color where the women stood. They could see the handkerchiefs flickering, until a turn of the channel swept them out of sight of the town, and they drifted on through the widening mouth of the bay, toward the open sea. At dusk that night, there was still land in sight behind them and on either side; but when Priscilla came on deck in the morning, there was nothing but blue water and laughing waves. And so she was homesick, all that day, and laughed not at all till the evening, when the moon bathed the ship in silver fire, and the white-caps danced all about them.

The *Nathan Ross* was in no sense a lovely ship. There was about her none of the poetry of the seas. She was designed strictly for utility, and for hard and dirty toil. Blunt she was of bow and stern, and her widest point was just abeam the fore-mast, so that she had great shoulders that buffeted the sea. These shoulders bent in-ward toward the prow and met in what was practically a right angle; and her stern was cut almost straight across, with only enough overhang to give the rudder room. Furthermore, her masts had no rake. They stood up stiff and straight as sore thumbs; and the bowsprit, instead of being something near horizontal, rose toward the skies at an angle close to forty-five degrees. This bowsprit made the *Nathan Ross* look as though she had just stubbed her toe. She carried four boats at the davits; and two spare craft, bottom up, on the boathouse just forward of the mizzenmast. Three of the four at the davits were on the starboard side, and since they were each thirty feet long, while the ship herself was scarce a hundred and twenty, they gave her a sadly cluttered and overloaded appearance. For the rest, she was painted black, with a white checkerboarding around the rail; and her sails were smeared and smutty with smoke from burning blubber scraps.

Nevertheless, she was a comfortable ship, and a dry one. She rode waves that would have swept a vessel cut on prouder lines; and she was moderately steady. She was not fast, nor cared to be. An easy five or six knots contented her; for the whole ocean was her hunting ground, and though there were certain more favored areas, you might meet whales anywhere. Give her time, and she would poke that blunt nose of hers right 'round the world, and come back with a net profit anywhere up to a hundred and fifty thousand dollars in her sweating casks.

Priscilla Holt knew all these things, and she respected the *Nathan Ross* on their account. But during the first weeks of the cruise, she was too much interested in the work on the cabin to consider other matters. Old Aaron Burnham, the car-penter, did the work. He was a wiry little man, gray and grizzled; and he loved the tools of his craft with a jealous love that forbade the laying on of impious hands.

Through the long, calm days, when the ship snored like a sleep-walker through the empty seas, Priscilla would sit on box or bench or floor, and watch Aaron at his task, and ask him questions, and listen to the old man's long stories of things that had come and gone.

Sometimes she tried to help him; but he would not let her handle an edged tool. "Ye'll no have the eye for it," he would say. "Leave it be." Now and then he let her try to drive a nail; but as often as not she missed the nail head and marred the soft wood, until Aaron lost patience with her. "Mark you," he cried, "men will see the scar there, and they'll be thinking I did this task with my foot, Ma'am."

And Priscilla would laugh at him, and curl up with her feet tucked under her skirts and her chin in her hands, and watch him by the long hour on hour.

The task dragged on; it seemed to her endless. For Aaron had other work that must be done, and he could give only his spare time to this. Also, he was a slow worker, accustomed to take his own time; and when Priscilla grew impatient and scolded him, the old man merely sat back on his knees, and scratched his head, and tapped thoughtfully with his hammer on the floor beside him.

"We-ell, Ma'am," he said, "I do things so, and I do things so; and it takes time, that does, Ma'am."

Now and then, through those days, Priscilla's enthusiasm would send her skittering up the companion to fetch Joel to see some new wonder--a window set in the stern, or a bench completed, or a door hung. And Joel, looking far oftener at Priscilla than at the object she wished him to consider, would chuckle, and touch her shoulder affectionately, and go back to his post.

In the sixth week, the last nail had been driven, and the last lick of paint was dry. In the result, Priscilla was as happy as a bride has a right to be.

Across the very stern of the ship, with windows looking out upon the wake, ran what might have been called a sitting room. It was perhaps twenty feet wide and eight feet deep; and its rear wall--formed by the overhanging stern--sloped outward toward the ceiling. Against this slope, beneath the three windows, a broad, cushioned bench was built, to serve as couch or seat. The bench was broken in one place to make room for Joel's desk, and the cabinet wherein he kept his records and his instruments. Priss had put curtains on the windows; and she had a lily, in a pot, at one of them, and a clump of pansies at another. Joel's cabin opened off this compartment, on the starboard side; hers was opposite. The main cabin, with its folding table built about the thick butt of the mizzenmast, had been extended forward to make room for the enlargement of this stern apartment; and the mates were quartered off this main cabin. The galley and the store rooms were on the main deck, in the after house, on either side of the awkward "walking wheel" by which the ship was steered; and the cabin companion was just forward of this wheel.

There were aboard the **Nathan Ross** about thirty men, all told; but the most of them were not of Priscilla's world. The foremast hands never came aft of the try works, save on tasks assigned; and the secondary officers--boat-steerers and the like--slept in the steerage and kept forward of the boathouse. Thus the after deck was shared only by Priscilla and Joel, the mates, the cook, and old Aaron, who was a man of many privileges.

This world, Priscilla ruled. Joel adored her; Jim Finch gave her the clumsy homage of a puppy--and was at times just as oppressively amiable. Old Aaron talked to her by the hour, while he went about his work. And the other mates--Varde, the sullen; and Hooper, who was old and losing his grip; and Dick Morrell, who was young and finding his--paid her the respect that was her due. Young Morrell--he was not even as old as she was--helped her on her first climb to the mast head. He was only a boy.... The girl, when the first homesick pangs were past, was happy.

Until the day they killed their whale, a seventy-barrel cachalot cow who died as peaceably as a chicken, with only a convulsive flop or two when the lances found the life. Priscilla took a single glimpse of the shuddering, bloody, oily work of cutting in the carcass, and then she fled to her cabin and remained there steadfastly until the long task was done. The smoke from the bubbling try pots, and the persistent smell of boiling blubber sickened her; and the grime that descended over everything appalled her dainty soul. Not until the men had cleaned ship did she go on deck again; and even then she scolded Joel for the affair as though it were a matter for which he was wholly to blame.

"There just isn't any sense in making so much dirt," she told him. "I've had to wash out every one of my curtains; and I can't ever get rid of that smell."

Joel chuckled. "Aye, the smell sticks," he agreed. "But you'll be used to it soon, Priss. You'll come to like it, I'm thinking. Any case, we'll not be rid of it while the cruise is on."

She was so angry that she wanted to cry. "Do you actually mean, Joel Shore, that I've got to live with that sickening, hot-oil smell for th-three years?"

He nodded slowly. "Yes, Priss. No way out of it. It's part of the work. Come another month, and you'll not mind at all."

She said positively: "I may not say anything, but I shall always hate that smell."

His eyes twinkled slowly; and she stamped her foot. "If I'd known it was going to be like this, I wouldn't have come, Joel. Now don't you laugh at me. If there was any way to go back, I'd go. I hate it. I hate it all. You ought not to have brought me...."

They were on the broad bench across the stern, in their cabin; and he put his big arm about her shoulders and laughed at her till she could do no less than laugh back at him. But--she assured herself of this--she was angry, just the same. Nevertheless, she laughed....

Joel had put the **Nathan Ross** on the most direct southward course, touching neither Azores nor Cape Verdes. For it was in his mind, as he had told Asa Worthen, to make direct for the Gilbert Islands and seek some trace of his brother there. That had been his plan before he left port; but the plan had become determination after a word with Aaron Burnham, one day. Joel, resting in the cabin while old Aaron worked there, fell to thinking of his brother, and so asked:

"Aaron, what is your belief about my brother, Mark Shore? Is he dead?"

Aaron was building, that day, the forward partition of the new cabin, fitting his boards meticulously, and driving home each nail with hammer strokes that seemed smooth and effortless, yet sank the nail to the head in an instant. He looked up over his shoulder at Joel, between nails.

"Dead, d'ye say?" he countered quizzically.

Joel nodded. "The Islanders? Did they do it, do you believe?"

Old Aaron chuckled asthmatically. He had lost a fore tooth, and the effect of his mirth was not reassuring. "There's a brew i' the Islands," he said. "More like 'twas the island brew nor the island men."

Joel, for a moment, sat very still and considered. He knew Mark Shore had never scrupled to take strong drink when he chose; but Mark had always been a strong man to match his drink, and conquer it. Said Joel, therefore, after a space of thought:

"Why do you think that, Aaron? Drink was never like to carry Mark away."

Aaron squinted up at him. "Have ye sampled that island brew? 'Tis made of pineapples, or sago, or the like outlandish stuff, I've heard. And one sip is deviltry, and two is madness, and three is corruption. Some stomachs are used to it; they can handle it. But a raw man...."

There was significance in the pause, and the unfinished sentence. Joel considered the matter. There had always been, between him and Mark, something of that sleeping enmity that so often arises between brothers. Mark was a man swift of tongue, flashing, and full of laughter and hot blood; a colorful man, like a splash of pigment on white canvas. Joel was in all things his opposite, quiet, and slow of thought and speech, and steady of gait. Mark was accustomed to jeer at him, to taunt him; and Joel, in the slow fashion of slow men, had resented this. Nevertheless, he cast aside prejudice now in his estimate of the situation; and he asked old Aaron:

"Do you know there were Islanders about? Or this wild brew you speak of?"

Aaron drove home a nail, and with his punch set it flush with the soft wood. "There was some drunken crew, shouting and screeching a mile up the beach," he said. "Some few of them came off to us with fruit. The sober ones. 'Twas them Mark Shore went to pandander with."

"He went to them?" Joel echoed. Aaron nodded.

"Aye. That he did."

There was a long moment of silence before Joel asked huskily: "But was it like that he should stay with them freely?" For it is a black and shameful thing that a captain should desert his ship. When he had asked the question, he waited in something like fear for the carpenter's answer.

"It comes to me," said Aaron slowly at last, "that you did not well know your brother. Ye'd only seen him ashore. And--I'm doubting that you knew all the circumstances of his departure from this ship."

"I know that he went ashore," said Joel. "Went ashore, and left his men, and departed; and I know that they searched for him three weeks without a sign."

Aaron sat back on his heels, and rubbed the smooth head of his hammer thoughtfully against his dry old cheek. "I'm not one to speak harm," he said. "And I've said naught, in the town. But--you have some right to know that Mark Shore was not a sober man when he left the ship. I' truth, he had not been sober--cold sober--for a week. And he left with a bottle in his coat." He nodded his gray old head, eyes not on Joel, but on the hammer in his hand. "Also, there was a pearling schooner in the lagoon, with drunk white men aboard."

He glanced sidewise at Joel then, and saw the Captain's cheek bones slowly whiten. Whereupon old Aaron bent swiftly to his task, half fearful of what he had said. But when Joel spoke, it was only to say quietly:

"Asa should have told me this."

Aaron shook his head vehemently, but without looking up from his task. "Not so," he said. "There was no need the town should chew Mark's name. Better--" He glanced at Joel. "Better if he were thought dead. Asa's a good man, you mind. And--he knew your father."

Joel nodded at that. "Asa meant wisest, I've no doubt," he agreed. "But--Mark would do nothing that he was shamed of."

"Mark Shore," said Aaron thoughtfully, "did many things without shame for which other men would have blushit."

Joel said curtly: "Aaron, ye'll say no more such things as that."

"Ye're right," Aaron agreed. "I should no have said it. But--'tis so."

Joel left him and went on deck, and his eyes were troubled.... Priss was there, with Dick Morrell showing her some trick of the wheel, and they were laughing together like children. Joel felt immensely older than Priss.... Yet the difference was scarce six years.... She saw him, and left Morrell and came running to Joel's side. "Did you sleep?" she asked. "You needed rest, Joe."

"I rested," he told her, smiling faintly. "I'll be fine...."

V

They drifted past Pernambuco, and touched at Trinidad, and so worked south and somewhat westward for Cape Horn. And in Joel grew, stronger and ever, the resolve to hunt out Mark, and find him, and fetch him home.... The blood tie was strong on Joel; stronger than any memory of Mark's derision. And--for the honor of the House of Shore, it were well to prove the matter, if Mark were dead. It is not well for a Shore to abandon his ship in strange seas.

He asked Aaron, two weeks after their first talk, whether they had questioned the white men on the pearling schooner.

"Oh, aye," said Aaron cheerfully. "I sought 'em out, myself. Three of them, they was; and ill-favored. A slinky small man, and a rat-eyed large man, and a fat man in between; all unshaven, and filthy, and drunken as owls. They'd seen naught of Mark Shore, they said. I'm thinking he'd let them see but little of him. He had no tenderness for dirt."

Joel told Priss nothing of what he hoped and feared; nor did he question Jim Finch in the matter. Finch was a good man at set tasks, but he was too amiable, and he had no clamp upon his lips.... Joel did not wish the word to go abroad among the men. He was glad that most of the crew were new since last voyage; but the officers were unchanged, save that he stood in his brother's shoes.

They left Trinidad behind them, and shouldered their way southward, the blunt bow of the **Nathan Ross** battering the seas. And they came to the Straits, and worked in, and made their westing day by day, while little Priss, wide-eyed on the deck, watched the gaunt cliffs past whose wave-gnawed feet they stole. And so at last the Pacific opened out before them, and they caught the winds, and worked toward Easter Island.

But their progress was slow. To men unschooled in the patience of the whaling trade, it would have been insufferably slow. For they struck fish; and day after day they hung idle on the waves while the trypots boiled; and day after day they loitered on good whaling grounds, when the boats were out thrice and four times between sun's rise and set. If Joel was impatient, he gave no sign. If his desires would have made him hasten on, his duty held him here, where rich catches waited for the taking; and while there were fish to be taken, he would not leave them behind.

Priscilla hated it. She hated the grime, and the smoke, and the smell of boiling oil; and she hated this dawdling on the open seas, with never a glimpse of land. More than once she made Joel bear the brunt of her own unrest; and because it is not always good for two people to be too much together, and because she had nothing better to do, she began to pick Joel to pieces in her thoughts, and fret at his patience and stolidity. She wished he would grow angry, wished even that he might be angry with her.... She wished for anything to break the long days of deadly calm. And she watched Joel more intently than it is well for wife to watch husband, or for husband to watch wife.

He did so many things that tried her sore. He had a fashion, when he had finished eating, of setting his hands against the table and pushing himself back from the board with slow and solid satisfaction. She came to the point where she longed to scream when he did this. When they were at table in the main cabin, she watched with such agony of trembling nerves for that movement of his that she forgot to eat, and could not relish what she ate.

Joel was a man, and his life was moving smoothly. His ship's casks were filling more swiftly than he had any right to hope; his wife was at his side; his skies were clear. He was happy, and comfortable, and well content. Sometimes, when they were preparing for sleep, at night, in the cabin at the stern, he would relax on the couch there. But she did not wish for him to put his feet upon the cushions; she said that his shoes were dirty. He offered to take off his shoes; and she shuddered....

He had a fashion of stretching and yawning comfortably as he bade her good night; and sometimes a yawn caught him in the middle of a word, and he talked while he yawned. She hated this. She was passing through that hard middle ground, that purgatory between maidenhood and wifehood in the course of which married folk find each other only human, after all. And she had not yet come to accept this condition, and to glory in it. She had always thought of Joel as a hero, a protector, a fine, stalwart, able, noble man. Now she forgot that he was commander of this ship and master of the men aboard her, and saw in him only a man who, when work was done, liked to take his ease--and who talked through his yawns.

She gnawed at this bone of discontent, in the hours when Joel was busy with his work. She was furiously resentful of Joel's flesh-and-bloodness.... And Joel, because he was too busy to be introspective, continued calmly happy and content.

The whales led them past Easter Island for a space; and then, abruptly, they were gone. Came day on day when the men at the masthead saw no misty spout against the wide blue of the sea, no glistening black body lying awash among the waves. And the Nathan Ross, with all hands scrubbing white the decks again, bent northward, working toward that maze of tiny islands which dots the wide South Seas.

Their water was getting stale, and running somewhat low; and they needed fresh foodstuffs. Joel planned to touch at the first land that offered. Tubuai, that would be. He marked their progress on the chart.

On the evening before they would reach the island, when Joel and Priss were preparing for sleep, Priss burst out furiously, like a teapot that boils over. The storm came without warning, and--so far as Joel could see--without provocation. She was sick, she said, of the endless wastes of blue. She wanted to see land. To step on it. If she were not allowed to do so very soon, she would die.

Joel, at first, was minded to tell her they would sight land in the morning; then, with one of the blundering impulses to which husbands fall victim at such moments, he decided to wait and surprise her. So, instead of telling her, he chuckled as though at some secret jest, and tried to quiet her by patting her dark head.

She fell silent at his caress; and Joel thought she was appeased. As a matter of fact, she was hating him for having laughed at her; and her calm was ferocious. He discovered this, too late....

He had just kissed her good night. She turned her cheek to his lips; and he was faintly hurt at this. But he only said cheerfully: "There, Priss.... You'll be all right in the morning...."

He yawned in mid-sentence, so that the last two or three words sounded as though he were trying to swallow a large and hot potato while he uttered them.

Priss could stand no more of that. Positively. So she slapped his face.

He was amazed; and he stood, looking at her helplessly, while the slapped cheek grew red and red. Priss burst into tears, stamped her foot, called him names she did not mean, and as a climax, darted into her own cabin, and swung the door, and snapped the latch.

Joel did not in the least understand; and he went to his bunk at last, profoundly troubled.

An hour after they anchored, the next day, at Tubuai, a boat came out from shore and ran alongside, and Mark Shore swung across the rail, aboard the *Nathan Ross*.

VI

Joel was below, in the cabin with Priss, when his brother boarded the ship. Varde and Dick Morrell had gone ashore for water and supplies, and Priss was to go that afternoon, with Joel. She was sewing a ribbon rosette upon the hat she would wear, when she and Joel heard the sound of excited voices, and the movement of feet on the deck above their head. He left her, curled up on the cushioned bench, with the gay ribbon in her hands, and went out through the main cabin, and up the companion. He had been trying, clumsily enough, to make friends with Priss; but she was very much on her dignity that morning....

When his head rose above the level of the cabin skylight, he saw a group of men near the rail, amidships. Finch, and Hooper, and old Aaron Burnham, and two of the harpooners, all pressing close about another man.... Finch obscured this other man from Joel's view, until he climbed up on deck. Then he saw that the other man was his brother.

He went forward to join them; and it chanced that at first no one of them looked in his direction. Mark's back was half-turned; but Joel could see that his brother was lean, and bronzed by the sun. And he wore no hat, and his thick, black hair was rumpled and wild. The white shirt that he wore was open at the throat above his brown neck. His arms were bare to the elbows. His chest was like a barrel. There was a splendor of strength and vigor about the man, in the very look of him, and in his eye, and his voice, and his laughter. He seemed to shine, like the sun....

Joel, as he came near them, heard Mark laugh throatily at something Finch had said; and he heard Finch say unctuously: "Be sure, Captain Shore, every man aboard here is damned glad you've come back to us. You were missed, missed sore, sir."

Mark laughed again, at that; and he clapped Jim's fat shoulder. The action swung him around so that he saw Joel for the first time. Joel thrust out his hand.

"Mark, man! They said you were dead," he exclaimed.

Mark Shore's eyes narrowed for an instant, in a quick, appraising scrutiny of his brother. "Dead?" he laughed, jeeringly. "Do I look dead?" He stared at Joel more closely, glanced at the other men, and chuckled. "By the Lord, kid," he cried, "I believe old Asa has put you in my shoes."

Joel nodded. "He gave me command of the *Nathan Ross*. Yes."

Mark looked sidewise at big Jim Finch, and grinned. "Over your head, eh, Jim? Too damned bad!"

Finch grinned. "I had no wish for the place, sir. You see, I felt very sure you would be coming back to your own."

Mark tilted back his head and laughed. "You were always a very cautious man, Jim Finch. Never jumped till you were sure where you would land." He wheeled on Joel. "Well, boy--how does it feel to wear long pants?"

Joel, holding his anger in check, said slowly: "We've done well. Close on eight hundred barrel aboard."

Mark wagged his head in solemn reproof. "Joey, Joey, you've been fiddling away your time. I can see that!"

Over his brother's shoulder, Joel saw the grinning face of big Jim Finch, and his eyes hardened. He said quietly: "If that's your tone, Mark, you'll call back your boat and go ashore."

A flame surged across Mark's cheek; and he took one swift, terrible step toward his brother. But Joel did not give ground; and after a moment in which their eyes clashed like swords, Mark relaxed, and laughed and bowed low.

"I was wrong, grievously wrong, Captain Shore," he said sonorously. "I neglected the respect due your office. Your high office, sir. I thank you for reminding me of the--the proprieties, Captain." And he added, in a different tone, "Now will you not invite me aft on your ship, sir?"

Joel hesitated for a bare instant, caught by a vague foreboding that he could not explain. But in the end he nodded, as though in answer to the unspoken question in his thoughts. "Will you come down into the cabin, Mark?" he invited quietly. "I've much to ask you; and you must have many things to tell."

Mark nodded. "I will come," he said; and his eyes lighted suddenly, and he dropped a hand on Joel's shoulder. "Aye, Joel," he said softly, into his brother's ear, as they went aft together. "Aye, I've much to tell. Many things and marvelous. Matters you'd scarce credit, Joel." Joel looked at him quickly, and Mark nodded. "True they are, Joel," he cried exultantly. "Marvelous--and true as good, red gold."

At the tone, and the eager light in his brother's eyes, Joel's slow pulses quickened, but he said nothing. At the top of the cabin companion, he stepped aside to let Mark descend first; and Mark went down the steep and awkward stair with the easy, sliding gait of a great cat. Joel, behind him, could see the muscles stir and swell upon his shoulders. In the cabin, Mark halted abruptly, and looked about, and exclaimed: "You've changed things, Joel. I'd not know the ship."

The door into Priscilla's cabin, across the stern, was open. Priss had finished that matter of the ribbon, and was watering her flowers, kneeling on the bench, when she heard Mark's voice, and knew it. And she cried, in surprise and joy: "Mark! Oh--Mark!" And she ran to the door, and stood there, framed for Mark's eyes against the light behind her, hands holding to the door frame on either side.

Mark cried delightedly: "Priss Holt!" And he was at her side in an instant, and caught her without ceremony, and kissed her roundly, as he had been accustomed to do when he came home from the sea. But he must have been a blind man not to have seen in that first moment that Priss was no longer child, but woman. And Mark was not blind. He kissed her till she laughingly fought herself free.

"Mark!" she cried again. "You're not dead. I knew you couldn't be...."

Joel, behind them, at sight of Priscilla in his brother's arms, had stirred with a quick rush of anger; but he was ashamed of it in the next moment, and stood still where he was. Mark held Priss by the shoulders, laughing down at her.

"And how did you know I couldn't be dead?" he demanded. "Miss Wise Lady."

She moved her head confusedly. "Oh--you were always so--so alive, or something.... You just couldn't be...."

He chuckled, released her, and stood away and surveyed her. "Priss, Priss," he said contritely, "you're not a little kid any longer. Dresses down, and hair up...." He wagged his head. "It's a wonder you did not slap my face." And then he looked from her to Joel, and abruptly he tossed his great head back and laughed aloud. "By the Lord," he roared. "The children are married. Married...."

Priscilla flushed furiously, and stamped her foot at him. "Of course we're married," she cried. "Did you think I'd come clear around the world with...." Her words were smothered in her own hot blushes, and Mark laughed again, until she cried: "Stop it. I won't have you laughing at us. Joel--make him stop!"

Mark sobered instantly, and he backed away from Joel in mock panic, both hands raised, defensively, so that they laughed at him. When they laughed, he cast aside his panic, and sat down on the cushions, stretching his legs luxuriously before him. "Now," he exclaimed. "Tell me all about it. When, and why, and how?"

Priss dropped on the bench beside him, feet tucked under her in the miraculous fashion of small women; and she enumerated her answers on the pink tips of her fingers. "When?" she repeated. "The day before we sailed. Why? Just because. How? In the same old way." She waved her hand, as though disposing of the matter once and for all, and looked up at him, and laughed. Joel thought she had not seemed so completely happy since the day the cabin was finished. "So," she said, "that's all there is to tell you about us. Tell us about you."

Mark's eyes twinkled. "Ah, now, what's the use? That will come later. Besides--some chapters are not for gentle ears." He nodded toward Joel. "So you love the boy, yonder?"

Priss bobbed her head, red lips pursed, eyes dancing.

"Why?" Mark demanded. "What do you discover in him?"

She looked at Joel, and they laughed together as though at some delightful secret, mutually shared. Mark wagged his head dolorously. "And I suppose he's wild about you?" he asked.

She nodded more vigorously than ever.

Mark rubbed his hands together. He looked at Joel, with a faintly malicious twinkle in his eyes. "Well, now!" he exclaimed. "That is certainly the best of news...." Joel saw the mocking and malignant little devil in his eye. "I've never had a kid sister," said Mark gayly. "And it's been the great sorrow of my life, Priss. So, Joel, you must expect Priss and myself to turn out the very best of friends."

And Priscilla, on the seat beside him, nodded her lovely head once more. "I should say so," she exclaimed.

VII

Mark Shore held something like a reception, on the **Nathan Ross**, all that first day. He went forward among the men to greet old friends and meet new ones, and came back and complimented Joel on the quality of his crew. "You've made good men of them," he said. "Those that weren't good men before."

He listened, with a smile half contemptuous, to Jim Finch's somewhat slavish phrases of welcome and admiration; and he talked with Varde, the morose second mate, so gayly that even Varde was cozened at last into a grin. Old Hooper was pathetically glad to see him. Hooper had been mate of the ship on which Mark started out as a boy; and he liked to hark back to those days. Young Dick Morrell, on his trips from the shore, gave Mark frank worship.

Joel saw all this. He could not help seeing it. And he told himself, again and again, that it was only to be expected. Mark had captained this ship, had captained these men, on their last cruise; they had thought him dead. It was only natural that they should welcome him back to life again....

But even while he gave himself this reassurance, he knew that it was untrue. There was more than mere welcome in the attitude of the men; there was more than admiration. There was a quality of awe that was akin to worship; and there was, beneath this awe, a lively curiosity as to what Mark would do.... They knew him for a quick man, dominant, one with the will to lead; and now he found himself supplanted, dependent on the word of his own younger brother.... Every one knew that Mark and Joel had always been rather enemies than comrades; so, now, they wondered, and waited, and watched with all their eyes. Joel saw them, by twos and threes, whispering together about the ship; and he knew what it was they were asking each other.

Of all those on the ***Nathan Ross*** that day, Mark himself seemed least conscious of the dramatic possibilities of the situation. He was glad to be back among friends; but beyond that he did not go. He gave Joel an exaggerated measure of respect, so extreme that it was worse than scorn or mockery. Otherwise, he took no notice of the potentialities created by his return.

Priss had planned to go ashore in the afternoon; but Mark dissuaded her. This was not difficult; he did it so laughingly and so dextrously that Priss changed her mind without knowing just why she did so. Mark took it upon himself to make up for her disappointment; they were together most of the long, hot afternoon. Joel could hear their laughter now and then.

He had expected to go ashore with Priss; but when she came to him and said: "Joel, Mark says it's just dirty and hot and ugly, ashore, and I'm not going," he changed his mind. There was no need of his making the trip, after all. Varde and Morrell had brought out water, towing long strings of almost-filled casks behind their boats; and boats from the shore had come off to sell fresh food. So at dusk, the anchor came up, and the ***Nathan Ross*** spread her dingy sails, and stalked out of the harbor with the utmost dignity in every stiff line of her, and the night behind them swallowed up the island. Mark and Priss were astern to watch it blend in the darkness and lose itself; and Priss, when their last glimpse of it faded, heard the man draw a deep breath of something like relief. She looked up at him with wide, curious eyes.

"What is it?" she asked softly. "Were you--unhappy there?"

Mark laughed aloud. "My dear Priss," he said, in the elder-brother manner he affected toward her. "My dear Priss, the South Sea Islands are no place for a white man, especially when he is alone. I'm glad to get back in the smell of oil, with an honest deck underfoot. And I don't mind saying so."

Priss shuddered, and wrinkled her nose. "Ugh, how I hate that smell," she exclaimed. "But, Mark--tell me where you've been, and what you did, and--everything. Why won't you tell?"

He wagged his head at her severely. "Children," he said, "should be seen and not heard."

She stamped her foot. "I'm not a child. I'm a woman."

He bent toward her suddenly, his dark eyes so close to hers that she could see the flickering flame which played in them, and the twist of his smile. "I wonder!" he whispered. "Oh--I wonder if you are...."

She was frightened, deliciously....

Mark had persisted, all day long, in his refusal to tell her of himself. He had dropped a sentence now and then that brought to life in her imagination a strange, wild picture.... But always he set a bar upon his lips, caught back the words, refused to explain what it was he had meant to say. When she persisted, he laughed at her and told her he only did it to be mysterious. "Mystery is always interesting, you understand," he explained. "And--I wish to be very interesting to you, Priss."

She looked around the after deck for Joel; but he was below in the cabin, and she decided, abruptly, that she must go down....

They had bought chickens at Tubuai, and they had two of them, boiled, for supper that night in the cabin. It was a feast, after the long months of sober diet; and the presence of Mark made it something more. He was a good talker, and without revealing anything of the months of his disappearance, he nevertheless told them stories that held each one breathless with interest. But after supper, he went on deck with Finch, and Joel and Priss sat in the cabin astern for a while; and Joel wrote up, in the ship's log, the story of his brother's return. Priss read it over his shoulder, and afterwards she clung close to Joel. "He's a terribly--overwhelming man, isn't he?" she whispered.

Joel looked down at her, and smiled thoughtfully. "Aye, Mark's a big man," he agreed. "Big--in many ways. But--you'll be used to him presently, Priss."

When she prepared to go to bed, he bade her good night and left her, and went on deck; and Priss, in her narrow bunk in the cabin at the side of the ship, lay wide-eyed with many thoughts stirring in her small head. She was still awake when she heard them come down into the main cabin together, Joel and Mark. The walls were thin; she could hear their words, and she heard Mark ask: "Sure Priss is asleep? There are parts--not for the pretty ears of a bride, Joel."

Priss was not asleep, but when Joel came to see, she closed her eyes, and lay as still as still, scarce breathing. Joel bent over her softly; and he touched her head, clumsily, with his hand, and patted it, and went away again, closing her door behind him. She heard him tell Mark: "Aye, she's fast asleep."

The brothers sat by Joel's desk, in the cabin across the stern; and Mark, without preamble, told his story there. Priss, ten feet away, heard every word; and she lay huddled beneath the blankets, eyes staring upward into the darkness of her cabin; and as she listened, she shuddered and trembled and shrank at the terror and wonder and ugliness of the tale he told. No Desdemona ever listened with such half-caught breath....

VIII

"Y̶ou're blaming me," said Mark, when he and Joel were puffing at their pipes, "for leaving my ship."

Joel said slowly: "No. But I do not understand it."

Mark laughed, a soft and throaty laugh. "You would not, Joel. You would not. For you never felt an overwhelming notion that you must dance in the moon upon the sand. You've never felt that, Joel; and--I have."

"I'm not a hand for dancing," said Joel.

Mark seemed to forget that his brother sat beside him. His eyes became misty and thoughtful, as though he were living over again the days of which he spoke. "Mind, Joel," he said, "there's a pagan in every man of us. And there's two pagans in some of us. And I'm minded, Joel, that there are three of them in me. 'Twas so, that night."

"It was night when you left the ship?"

"Aye, night. Night, and the moon; and it may have been that I had been drinking a drop or two. Also, as you shall see, I was not well. I tell these things, not by way of excuse and palliation; but only so that you may understand. D'ye see? I was three pagans in one body, and that body witched by moon, and twisted by drink, and trembling with fever. And so it was I went ashore, and flung my men behind me, and went off, dancing, along the hard sand.

"That was a night, Joel. A slow-winded, warm, trembling night when there was a song in the very air. The wind tingled on your throat like a woman's finger tips; and the sea was singing at the one side, and the wind in the palms on the other. And ahead of me, the wild, discordant chanting of the Islanders about their fires.... That singing it was that got me by the throat, and led me. I twirled around and around, very solemnly, by myself in the moonlight on the sand; and all the time I went onward toward the fires....

"I remember, when I came in sight of the fires, I threw away my coat and ran in among them. And they scattered, and yelled their harsh, meaningless, throaty yells. And they hid in the bush to stare at me by the fire.... They hid in the rank, thick grasses. All except one, Joel."

Joel, listening, watched his brother and saw through his brother's eyes; for he knew, for all his slow blood, the witchery of those warm, southern nights.

"The moon was on her," said Mark. "The moon was on her, and there was a red blossom in her hair, and some strings of things that clothed her. A little brown girl, with eyes like the eyes of a deer. And--not afraid of me. That was the thing that got me, Joel. She stood in my path, met me, watched me; and her eyes were not afraid....

"She was very little. She was only a child. I suppose we would call her sixteen or seventeen years old. But they ripen quickly, Joel--these Island children. Her little shoulders were as smooth and soft.... You could not even mark the ridge of her collar bones, she was fleshed so sweetly. She stood, and watched me; and the others crept out of the grasses, at last, and stood about us. And then this little brown girl held up her hand to me, and pointed me out to the others, and said something. I did not know what it was that she said; but I know now. She said that I was sick.

"I did not know then that I was sick. When she lifted her hand to me, I caught it; and I began to lead her in a wild dance, in the moonlight, about their dying fires. I could see them, in the shadows, their eyeballs shining as they watched us.... And they seemed, after a little, to move about in a misty, inhuman fashion; and they twisted into strange, cloud-like shapes. And I stopped to laugh at them, and my head dropped down before I could catch it and struck against the earth, and the earth forsook me, Joel, and left me swimming in nothing at all....

"My memory was a long time in coming back to me, Joel. It would peep out at me like a timid child, hiding among the trees. I would see it for an instant; then 'twould be gone. But I know it must have been many days that I was on the island there. And I knew, after a time, that I was most extremely sick; and the little brown girl put cool leaves on my head, and gave me strange brews to drink, and rubbed and patted my chest and my body with her hands in a fashion that was immensely comfortable and strengthening. And I twisted on a bed of coarse grass.... And I remember singing, at times...."

He looked toward Joel, eyes suddenly flaming. "Eh, Joel, I tell you I was not three pagans, but six, in those days. The thing's clear beyond your guessing, Joel. But it was big. An immense thing. I was back at the beginning of the world, with food, and drink, and my woman.... It was big, I tell you. Big!"

His eyes clouded--he fell silent, and so at last went on again. "I was asleep one night, tossing in my sleep. And something woke me. And I laid my hand on the spot beside me where the little brown girl used to lie, and she was gone. So I got up, unsteadily. There were rifles snapping in the night; and there were screams. And I heard a white man's black curse; and the slap of a blow of flesh on flesh. And the screams.

"So I went that way; and the sounds retreated before me, until I came out, un-steadily, upon the open beach. There was no moon, that night; and the water of the lagoon was shot with fire. And there was a boat, pulling away from the beach, with screaming in it.

"I swam after the boat for a long time, for I thought I had heard the voice of the little brown girl. The water was full of fire. When I lifted my arms, the fire ran down them in streams and drops. And sometimes I forgot what I was about, and stopped to laugh at these drops of fire. But in the end, I always swam on. I remember once I thought the little brown girl swam beside me, and I tried to throw my arm about her, and she wrenched away, and she burned me like a brand. I found, afterwards, what that was. My breast and sides were rasped and raw where a shark's rough skin had scraped them. I've wondered, Joel, why the beast did not take me....

"But he did not; for I bumped at last into the boat, and climbed into it, and it was empty. But I saw a rope at the end of it, and I pulled the rope, and came to the schooner's stern, and climbed aboard her."

His voice was ringing, exultantly and proudly. "I swung aboard," he said. "And I stumbled over fighting bodies on the deck, astern there. And some one cried out, in the waist of her; and I knew it was the little brown girl. So I left those struggling bodies at the stern, for they were not my concern; and I went forward to the waist. And I found her there.

"A fat man had her. She was fighting him; and he did not see me. And I put my fingers quietly into his neck, from behind; and when he no longer kicked back at me, and no longer tore at my fingers with his, I dropped him over the side. I saw a fiery streak in the water where I dropped him. That shark was not so squeamish as the one I had--embraced. It may have been the other was embarrassed at my ways, Joel. D'ye think that might have been the way of it?"

Joel's knuckles were white, where his hand rested on his knee. Mark saw, and laughed softly. "There's blood in you, after all, boy," he applauded. "I've hopes for you."

Joel said slowly: "What then? What then, Mark?"

Mark laughed. "Well, that was a very funny thing," he said. "You see, the other two men, they were busy, astern, with their own concerns. And when I had comforted the little brown girl, and sat down on the deck to laugh at the folly of it all, she slipped away from me, and went aft, and got all their rifles. She brought them to me. She seemed to expect things of me. So I, still laughing, for the fever was on me; I took the rifles and threw them, all but one, over the side. And I went down into the cabin, with the little brown girl, and went to bed; and she sat beside me, with the rifle, and a lamp hanging above the door....

"And that was all that happened, until I woke one morning and saw her there, and wondered where I was. And my head was clear again. She made me understand that the men had sought to come at me, but had feared the rifle in her hands....

"And we were in the open sea, as I could feel by the labor of the schooner underfoot. So I took the rifle in the crook of my arm, and with the little brown girl at my heel, I went up on deck. And we made a treaty."

He fell silent for a moment, and Joel watched him, and waited. And at last, Mark went on.

"I had been more than a month on the island," he said. "The **Nathan Ross** had gone. This schooner was a pearler, and they had the location of a bed of shell. They had been waiting till another schooner should leave the place, to leave their own way clear. And when that time came, they went ashore to get the brown women for companions on that cruise. And they made the mistake of picking up my little brown girl, when she ran out of the hut. And so brought me down upon them.

"There were two of them left; two whites, and three black men forward, who were of no account. And the other two women. These other two were chattering together, on the deck astern, when I appeared. They seemed content enough...."

"The men were not happy. There was a large man with slanting eyes. There was Oriental blood in him. You could see that. He called himself Quint. But his eyes were Jap, or Chinese; and he had their calm, blank screen across his countenance, to hide what may have been his thoughts. Quint, he called himself. And he was a big man, and very much of a man in his own way, Joel.

"The other was little, and he walked with a slink and a grin. His name was Fetcher. And he was oily in his speech.

"When they saw me, they studied me for a considerable time without speech. And I stood there, with the rifle in my arm, and laughed at them. And at last, Quint said calmly:

"'You took Farrell.'

"'The fat man?' I asked him. He nodded. 'Yes,' I said. 'He took my girl, and so I dropped him into the water, and a friend met him there and hurried him away.'

"'Your girl?' he echoed, in a nasty way. 'You're that, then?'

"'Am I?' I asked, and shifted the rifle a thought to the fore. And his eyes held mine for a space, and then he shook his head.

"'I see that I was mistaken,' he said.

"'Your sight is good,' I told him. 'Now--what is this? Tell me.'

"He told me, evenly and without malice. They had a line on the pearls; there were enough for three. I was welcome. And at the end, I nodded my consent. The ***Nathan Ross*** was gone. Furthermore, there were nine pagans in me now; and the prospect of looting some still lagoon, in company with these two rats, had a wild flavor about it that caught me. My blood was burning; and the sun was hot. Also, they had liquor aboard her. Liquor, and loot, and the three women. Pagan, Joel. Pagan! But wild and red and raw. There's a glory about such things.... Songs are made of them.... There was no handshaking; but we made alliance, and crowded on sail, and went on our way."

He stopped short, laughed, filled his pipe again, watched Joel. "You're shocked with me, boy. I can see it," he taunted mockingly. Joel shook his head. "Will you hear the rest?" Mark asked; and Joel nodded. Mark lighted his pipe, laughed.... His fingers thrummed on the desk beside him.

"We were a week on the way," he said. "And all pagan, every minute of the week. Days when we fought a storm--as bad as I've ever seen, Joel. We fought it, holding to the ropes with our teeth, bare to the waist, with the wind scourging us. It tore at us, and lashed at us.... And we drove the three black men with knives to their work. And the three women stayed below, except my little brown girl. She came up, now and then, with dry clothes for me.... And I had to drive her to shelter....

"And when there was not the storm, there was liquor; and they had cards. We staked our shares in the catch that was to come.... Hour on hour, dealing, and playing with few words; and our eyes burned hollow in their sockets, and Quint's thin mouth twisted and writhed all the time like a worm on a pin. He was a nervous man, for all his calm. A very nervous man....

"The fifth day, one of the blacks stumbled in Quint's path, on deck. Quint had been losing, at the cards. He slid a knife from his sleeve into the man's ribs, and tipped the black over the rail without a word. I was twenty feet away, and it was done before I could catch breath. I shouted; and Quint turned and looked at me, and he smiled.

"'What is it?' he asked. 'Have you objections to present?' And the smeared blade in his hand, and the bubbles still rising, overside. I was afraid of the man, Joel. I tell you I was afraid. The only time. Fear's a pagan joy, boy. It was like a new drink to me. I nursed it, eating it. And I shook my head, humble.

"'No objections,' I said, to Quint. ''Tis your affair.'

"'That was my thought,' he agreed, and passed me, and went astern. I stood aside to let him pass, and trembled, and laughed for the joy of my fear.

"And then we came to the lagoon, and the blacks began to dive. Only the two we had; and there was no sign of Islanders, ashore. But the water was shallow, and we worked the men with knives, and they got pearls. Sometimes one or two in a day; sometimes a dozen. Do you know pearls, Joel? They're sweet as a woman's skin. I had never seen them, before. And we all went a little mad over them....

"They made Fetcher hysterical. He laughed too much. They made Quint morose. They made me tremble...."

He wiped his hand across his eyes, as though the memory wearied him; and he moved his great shoulders, and looked at Joel, and laughed. "But it could not last, in that fashion," he said. "It might have been anything. It turned out to be the women. I said they seemed content. They did. But that may be the way of the blacks. They have a happy habit of life; they laugh easily....

"At any rate, we found one morning that Quint's girl was gone. She was not on the schooner; and ashore, we found her tracks in the sand. She had gone into the trees. And we beat the island, and we did not find her. And Quint sweated. All that day.

"That night, he looked at my little brown girl, and touched her shoulder. I was across the deck, the girl coming to me with food. I said to him: 'No. She's mine, Quint.' And he looked at me, and I beat him with my eyes. And as his turned from mine, Fetcher and his woman came on deck, and Quint tapped Fetcher, and said to him: 'What will you take for her?'

"Fetcher laughed at him; and Quint scowled. And I--for I was minded to see sport, came across to them and said: 'Play for her. Play for her!'

"Fetcher was willing; because he had the blood that gambles anything. Quint was willing, because he was the better player. They sat down to the game, in the cabin, after supper. Poker. Cold hands. Nine of them. Winner of five to win....

"Fetcher got two, lost four, got two more. I was dealing. Card by card, face up-ward. I remember those hands. And my little brown girl, and the other, watching from the corner.

"The hands on the table grew, card by card. Fetcher got an ace, Quint a deuce. Fetcher a queen, Quint a seven. Fetcher a jack, Quint a six. Fetcher a ten, Quint a ten. Only the last card to come to each. If Fetcher paired any card, he would win. His card came first. It was a seven. He was ace, queen high. Quint had deuce, six, seven, ten. He had to get a pair to win....

"I saw Quint's hand stir, beneath the table; and I glimpsed a knife in it. But before I could speak, or stir, Fetcher dropped his own hand to his trouser leg, and I knew he kept a blade there.... So I laughed, and dealt Quint's last card....

"A deuce. He had a pair, enough to win....

"He leaned back, laughing grimly; and Fetcher's knife went in beneath the left side of his jaw, where the jugular lies. Quint looked surprised, and got up out of his chair and lay down quietly across the table. I heard the bubbling of his last breath.... Then Fetcher laughed, and called his woman, and they took Quint on deck and tipped him overside. The knife had been well thrown. Fetcher had barely moved his wrist.... I was much impressed with the little man, and told my brown girl so. But she was frightened, and I comforted her."

He was silent again for a time, pressing the hot ashes in his pipe with his thumb. The water slapped the broad stern of the ship beneath them, and Joel's pipe was gurgling. There was no other sound. Little Priss, nails biting her palms, thought she would stream if the silence held an instant more....

But Mark laughed softly, and went on.

"Fetcher and I worked smoothly together," he said. "The little man was very pleasant and affable; and I met him half way. The blacks brought up the shells, and we idled through the days, and played cards at night. We divided the take, each day; so our stakes ran fairly high. But luck has a way of balancing. On the day when we saw the end in sight, we were fairly even....

"Fetcher, and the blacks and I went ashore to get fruit from the trees there. Plenty of it everywhere; and we were running short. We went into the brush together, very pleasantly; and he fell a little behind. I looked back, and his knife brushed my neck and quivered in a tree a yard beyond me. So I went back and took him in my hands. He had another knife--the little man fairly bristled with them. But it struck a rib, and before he could use it again, his neck snapped.

"So that I was alone on the schooner, with the two blacks, and Fetcher's woman, and the little brown girl.

"Fetcher's woman went ashore to find him and never came back. And I decided it was time for me to go away from that place. The pagans were dying in me. I did not like that quiet little island any more.

"But the next morning, when I looked out beyond the lagoon, another schooner was coming in. So I was uncomfortable with Fetcher's pearls, as well as mine, in my pocket. There are some hard men in these seas, Joel; and I knew none of them would treasure me above my pearls. So I planned a story of misfortune, and I went ashore to hide my pearls under a rock.

"The blacks had brought me ashore. I went out of their sight to do what I had to do; and when I came back, after hiding the pearls, I saw them rowing very swiftly toward the schooner. And they looked back at me in a fearful way. I wondered why; and then four black men came down on me from behind, with knives and clubs.

"I had a very hard day, that day. They hunted me back and forth through the island--I had not even a knife with me--and I met them here and there, and suffered certain contusions and bruises and minor cuts. Also, I grew very tired of killing them. They were wiry, but they were small, and died easily. So I was glad, when from a point where they had cornered me I saw the little brown girl rowing the big boat toward me.

"She was alone. The blacks were afraid to come, I thought. But I found afterward that this was not true. They could not come; for they had tried to seize the schooner and go quickly away from that place, and the little brown girl had drilled them both. She had a knack with the rifle....

"I waded to meet the boat, and she tossed me the gun. I held them off for a little, while we drew away from the shore. But when we were thirty or forty yards off, I heard rifles from the other schooner, firing past us at the blacks in the bush; and the girl stopped rowing. So I turned around and saw that one of the balls from the other schooner had struck her in the back. So I sat there, in the sun, drifting with the wind, and held her in my arms till she coughed and died.

"Then I went out to the other schooner and told them they were bad marksmen. They had only been passing by, for copra; and the story I told them was a shocking one. They were much impressed, and they seemed glad to get away. But the blacks were still on shore, so that I could not go back for the pearls; and I worked the schooner out by myself, and shaped a course....

"I came to Tubuai, alone thus, a day before you, Joel."

IX

For a long time after Mark's story ended, the two brothers sat still in the cabin, puffing at their pipes, thinking.... Mark watched Joel, waiting for the younger man to speak. And Joel's thoughts ranged back, and picked up the tale in the beginning, and followed it through once more....

They were silent for so long that little Priss, in the cabin, drifted from waking dreams to dreams in truth. The pictures Mark's words had conjured up merged with troubled phantasies, and she twisted and cried out softly in her sleep so that Joel went in at last to be sure she was not sick. But while he stood beside her, she passed into quiet and untroubled slumber, and he came back and sat down with Mark again.

"You brought the schooner into Tubuai?" he asked.

"Aye. Alone. Half a thousand miles. There's a task, Joel."

"And left it there?"

"Yes."

"Why?"

Mark smiled grimly. "It was known there," he said quietly. "Also, the three whom I had found aboard it were known. And they had friends in Tubuai, who wondered what had come to them. I was beginning to--find their questions troublesome--when the **Nathan Ross** came in."

"They will ask more questions now," said Joel.

"They must ask them of the schooner; and--she does not speak," Mark told him.

Joel was troubled and uncertain. "It's--a black thing," he said.

"They'll not be after me, if that distresses you," Mark promised him. "Curiosity does not go to such lengths in these waters."

"You told no one?"

Mark laughed. "The pearls were--my own concern. You're the first I've told." He watched his brother. Joel frowned thoughtfully, shook his head.

"You plan to go back for them?" he asked.

"You and I," said Mark casually. Joel looked at him in quick surprise; and Mark laughed. "Yes," he repeated. "You and I. I am not selfish, Joel. Besides--there are plenty for two."

Joel, for an instant, found no word; and Mark leaned quickly toward him. He tapped Joel's knee. "We'll work up that way," he said quietly. "When we come to the island, you and I go ashore, and get them where they're hid beneath the rock; and we come back aboard with no one any wiser.... Rich. A double handful of them, Joel...."

Joel's eyes were clouded with thought; he shook his head slowly. "What of the blacks?" he asked.

Mark laughed. "They were brought down on us by the woman who got away," he said. "Quint's woman. I heard as much that day, saw her among them. But-- they're gone before this."

Joel said slowly: "You are not sure of that. And--I cannot risk the ship...."

Mark asked sneeringly: "Are you afraid?"

The younger man flushed; but he said steadily: "Yes. Afraid of losing Asa Worthen's ship for him."

Mark chuckled unpleasantly. "I'm minded of what is written, here and there, in the 'Log of the House of Shore,'" he said, half to himself. And he quoted: "'All the brothers were valiant....' There's more to that, Joel. 'And all the sisters virtuous.' I had not known we had sisters--but it seems you're one, boy. Not valiant, by your own admission; but at least you're fairly virtuous."

Joel paid no heed to the taunt. "Asa Worthen likes care taken of his ship," he said, half to himself. "I'm thinking he would not think well of this.... He's not a man to gamble...."

"Gamble?" Mark echoed scornfully. "He has no gamble in this. The pearls are for you and me. He will know nothing whatever about them. A handful for me, and a handful for you, Joel. For the taking...."

"You did not think to give him owner's lay?" Joel asked.

"No."

"Where is this island?"

Mark laughed. "I'll not be too precise--until I have your word, Joel. But--'tis to the northward."

"Our course is west, then south."

"Since when has the **Nathan Ross** kept schedule and time table like a mail ship?"

Joel shook his head. "I cannot do it, Mark."

"Why not?"

"A risk I have no right to take; and wasted weeks, out of our course. For which Asa Worthen pays."

Mark smiled sardonically. "You're vastly more virtuous than any sister could be, Joel, my dear."

Joel said steadily: "There may be two minds about that. There may be two minds as to--the duty of a captain to his ship and his owner. But--I've shown you my mind in the matter."

Mark leaned toward him, eyes half-friendly. "You're wrong, Joel. I'll convince you."

"You'll not."

"A handful of them," Mark whispered. "Worth anything up to a hundred thousand. Maybe more. I do not know the little things as well as some. All for a little jog out of your way...."

Joel shook his head. And Mark, in a sudden surge of anger, stormed to his feet with clenched hand upraised. "By the Lord, Joel, I'd not have believed it. You're mad; plain mad--sister, dear! You...."

Joel said quietly: "Your schooner is at Tubuai. I'll set you back there, if you will."

Mark mocked him. "Would you throw your own brother off the ship he captained?... Oh hard, hard heart...."

"You may stay, or go," Joel told him. "Have your way."

Mark's eyes for an instant narrowed; they turned toward the door of the cabin where Priss lay.... And there was a flicker of black hatred in them, but his voice was suave when he replied: "With your permission, captain dear, I'll stay."

Joel nodded; he rose. "Young Morrell has given you his bunk," he said. "So--good night, to you."

He opened the door into the main cabin; and Mark, his fingers twitching, went out. He turned, spoke over his shoulder. "Good night; and--pleasant dreams," he said.

X

Even Joel Shore saw the new light in Priscilla's eyes when she met Mark at breakfast in the cabin next morning; and it is said husbands are the last to see such things.

That story she had heard the night before, the story Mark told Joel in the after cabin, had made of him something superhuman in her eyes. He was a gigantic, an epic figure; he had lived red life, and fought for his life, and killed.... There was Puritan blood in Priscilla; but overrunning it was a flood of warmer life, a cross-strain from some southern forebear, which sang now in answer to the touch of Mark's words. She watched him, that morning, with wide eyes that were full of wonder and of awe.

Mark saw, and was immensely amused. He asked her: "Why do you look at me like that, little sister? I'm not going to bite...."

Priscilla caught herself, and smiled, and laughed at him. "How do I look at you? You're--imagining things, Mark."

"Am I?" he asked. And he touched Joel's arm. "Look at her, Joel, and see which of us is right."

Joel was eating his breakfast silently, but he had seen Priscilla's eyes. He looked toward her now, and she flushed in spite of herself, and got up quickly, and slipped away.... They watched her go, Joel's eyes clouded thoughtfully, Mark's shining. And when she was gone, Mark leaned across and said to Joel softly, a devil of mischief in his eyes: "She heard my tale last night, Joel. She was not asleep. Fooled you...."

Joel shook his head. "No. She was asleep."

Mark laughed. "Don't you suppose I know. I've seen that look in woman's eyes before. In the eyes of the little brown girl, the night I dropped the fat man over-side...."

He sat there, chuckling, when Joel got abruptly to his feet and went on deck; and when he came up the companion a little later, he was still chuckling under his breath.

After that first morning, Priss was able to cloak her eyes and hide her thoughts; and on the surface, life aboard the **Nathan Ross** seemed to go on as before. Mark threw himself into the routine of the work, mixing with the men, going off in the boats when there was a whale to be struck, doing three men's share of toil. Joel one day remonstrated with him. "It is not wise," he said. "You were captain here; you are my brother. It is not wise for you to mix, as an equal, with the men."

Mark only laughed at him. "Your dignity is very precious to you, Joel," he mocked. "But as for me--I am not proud. You'd not have me sit aft and twiddle my thumbs and hold yarn for little Priss.... And I must be doing something...."

He and Jim Finch were much together. Finch always gave Joel careful obedience, always handled the ship when he was in charge with smooth efficiency. His boat was the best manned and the most successful of the four. But he and Joel were not comradely. Joel instinctively disliked the big man; and Finch's servility disgusted him. The mate was full of smooth and flattering words, but his eyes were shallow.

Mark talked with him long, one morning; and then he left Finch and came to Joel, by the after house, chuckling as though at some enormous jest. "Will ye look at Finch, there?" he begged.

Joel had been watching the two. He saw Finch now, standing just forward of the boat house with flushed cheeks and eyes fixed and hands twitching. The big man was powerfully moved by something.... "What is it that's got him?" Joel asked.

"I've told him about the pearls," Mark chuckled. "He's wild to be after them...."

Joel turned on his brother hotly. "You're mad, Mark," he snapped. "That is no word to be loose in the ship."

"I've but told Finch," Mark protested. "It's mirthful to watch the man wiggle."

"He'll tell the ship. His tongue wags unceasingly."

Mark lifted his shoulders. "Tell him to be silent. You should keep order on your ship, Joel."

Joel beckoned, and Finch came toward them. As he came, he fought for self control; and when he stood before them, his lips were twisting into something like a smile, and his eyes were shifty and gleaming. Joel said quietly:

"Mr. Finch, my brother says he has told you his story."

"Yes, sir," said Finch. "An extraordinary adventure, Captain Shore."

"I think it best the men should know nothing about it," Joel told him. "You will please keep it to yourself."

Finch grinned. "Of course, sir. There's no need they should have any share in them."

Joel flushed angrily. "We are not going after them. I consider it dangerous, and unwise."

Over Finch's fat cheeks swept a twitching grimace of dismay. "But I thought...." He looked at Mark, and Mark was chuckling. "It's so easy, sir," he protested. "Just go, and get them.... Rich...."

Joel shook his head. "Keep silent about the matter, Finch."

Finch slowly bowed his head, and he smirked respectfully. "Very well, Captain Shore," he agreed. "You always know best, sir."

He turned away; and after a little Mark said softly: "You have him well trained, Joel. Like a little dog.... I wonder that you can handle men so...."

Two days later, Joel knew that either Finch or Mark had told the tale anew. Young Dick Morrell came to him with shining eyes. "Is it true, sir, that we're going after the pearls your brother hid?" he asked. "I just heard...."

Joel gripped the boy's arm. "Who told you?"

Morrell twisted free, half angry. "I--overheard it, sir. Is it true?"

"No," said Joel. "We're a whaler, and we stick to our trade."

Dick lifted both hands, in a gesture almost pleading. "But it would be so simple, sir...."

"Keep the whole matter quiet, Morrell," Joel told him. "I do not wish the men to know of it. And if you hear any further talk, report it to me."

Morrell's eyes were sulky. He said slowly: "Yes, sir." The set of his shoulders, as he stalked forward, seemed to Joel defiant....

Within the week, the whole ship knew the story. Old Aaron Burnham, repairing a bunk in the fo'c's'le, heard the men whispering the thing among themselves. "Tongues hissing like little serpents, sir," he told Joel, in the cabin that night. "All of pearls, and women, and the like.... And a shine in their eyes...."

"Thanks, Aaron," Joel said. "I'm sorry the men know...."

"Aye, they know. Be sure of that," Aaron repeated, with bobbing head. "And they're roused by what they know. Some say you're going after the pearls, and aim to fraud them of their lay. And some say you're a mad fool that will not go...."

Joel's fist, on the table, softly clenched. "What else?" he asked.

Aaron watched him sidewise. "There was a whisper that you might be made to go...."

Priscilla saw, that night, that Joel was troubled. She and Mark were together on the cushioned seat in the after cabin, and Joel sat at his desk, over the log. Mark was telling Priss an expurgated version of some one of his adventures; and Joel, looking once or twice that way, saw the quick-caught breath in her throat, saw her tremulous interest.... And his eyes clouded, so that when Priscilla chanced to look toward him, she saw, and cried:

"Joel! What's the matter? You look so...."

He looked from one of them to the other for a space; and then his eyes rested on Mark's, and he said slowly: "It's in my mind that I'd have done best to set you ashore at Tubuai, Mark."

Mark laughed; but Priss cried hotly: "Joel! What a perfectly horrible thing to say!" Her voice had grown deeper and more resonant of late, Joel thought. It was no longer the voice of a girl, but of a woman.... Mark touched her arm.

"Don't care about him," he told her. "That's only brotherly love...."

"He oughtn't to say it."

Joel said quietly: "This is a matter you do not understand, Priscilla. You would do well to keep silent. It is my affair."

A month before, this would have swept Priss into a fury of anger; but this night, though her eyes burned with slow resentment, she bit her lips and was still. A month ago, she would have forgotten over night. Now she would remember....

Mark got up, laughed. "He's bad company, Priss," he told her. "Come on deck with me."

She rose, readily enough; and they went out through the main cabin, and up the companionway. Joel watched them go. They left open the door into the cabin, and he heard Varde and Finch, at the table there, talking in husky whispers.... It was so, he knew, over the whole ship. Everywhere, the men were whispering.... There hung over the *Nathan Ross* a cloud as definite as a man's hand; and every man scowled--save Mark Shore. Mark smiled with malicious delight at the gathering storm he had provoked....

Joel, left in the after cabin, felt terribly lonely. He wanted Priss with him, laughing, at his side. His longing for her was like a hot coal in his throat, burning there. And she had taken sides with Mark, against him.... His shoulders shook with the sudden surge of his desire to grip Mark's lean throat.... Ashore, he would have done so. But as things were, the ship was his first charge; and a break with Mark would precipitate the thing that menaced the ship.... He could not fight Mark without risking the *Nathan Ross*; and he could not risk the *Nathan Ross*. Not even.... His head dropped for an instant in his arms, and then he got up quickly, and shook himself, and set his lips.... No man aboard must see the trouble in his heart....

He went through the main cabin, and climbed to the deck. There was some sea running, and a wind that brushed aside all smaller sounds, so that he made little noise. Thus, when he reached the top of the companion, he saw two dark figures in the shadows of the boat house, closely clasped....

He stood for an instant, white hot.... His wife, and Mark.... His little Priss, and his brother....

Then he went quietly below, and glanced at the chart, and chose a course upon it. The nearest land; he and Mark ashore together.... His blood ran hungrily at the thought....

XI

Priscilla went on deck that night so angry with Joel that she could have killed him; and Mark played upon her as a skilled hand plays upon the harp. It was such a night as the South Seas know, warm and languorous, the wind caressing, and the salt spray stinging gently on the cheek. The moon was near the full, and it laid a path of silver on the water. This path was like the road to fairyland; and Mark told Priscilla so. He dropped into a gay little phantasy that he conceived on the moment, a story of fairies, and of dancing in the moonlight, and of a man and a woman, hand in hand....

She felt the spell he laid upon her, and struggled against it. "Tell me about the last fight, when the little brown girl was killed," she begged.

He had told her snatches of his story here and there; but he had not, till that night, spoken of the pearls. When Priss heard of them, she swung about and lifted up her face to his, listening like a child. And Mark told the story with a tongue of gold, so that she saw it all; the lagoon, blue in the sun; and the schooner creeping in from the sea; and the hours of flight through the semi-jungle of the island, with the blacks in such hot pursuit. He told her of the times when they surrounded him, when he fought himself free.... How he got a great stone and gripped it in his hand, and how with this stone he crushed the skull of a young black with but one eye. Priss shuddered with delicious horror at the tale....

She loved best to hear of the little brown girl whom Mark had loved; and that would have told either of them, if they had stopped to consider, that she did not love Mark. Else she would have hated the other, brown or white.... And he told how the brown girl saved him, and gave her life in the saving, and how he had stopped at a little atoll on his homeward way and buried her.... She had died in his arms, smiling because she lay there....

"And the pearls?" Priss asked, when she had heard the story through. "You left them there?"

"There they are still," he told her. "Safely hid away."

"How many?" she asked. "Are they lovely?"

"Three big ones, and thirty-two of a fair size, and enough little ones and seeds to make a double handful."

"But why did you leave them there?"

"The black men were on the island. They were there, and watchful, and very angry."

"Couldn't you have kept them in your pocket?"

He laughed. "That other schooner made me cautious. Man's life is cheap, in such matters. And if they guessed I had such things upon me.... If I slept too sound-ly, or the like.... D'ye see?"

She nodded her dark head. "I see. But you'll go back...."

He chuckled at that, and tapped on the rail with one knuckle, in a thoughtful way. "I had thought that Joel and I would go, in the *Nathan Ross*, and fetch the things away," he said.

"Of course," she exclaimed. "That would be so easy.... I'd love to see the-- pearls...."

"Easy? That was my own thought," he agreed. Something in his tone prompted her question.

"Why--isn't it?"

"Joel objects," he said drily.

"He--won't. But why? I don't understand. Why?"

Mark laughed. "He speaks of a matter of duty, not to risk the ship."

"Is there a risk?"

"No." He chuckled maliciously. "As a matter of cold fact, Priss, I'm fearful that Joel is a bit--timid in such affairs."

She flamed at him: "Afraid?"

He nodded.

"I don't believe it."

His eyes shone. "What a loyal little bride? But--I taxed him with it. And--that was the word he used...."

She was so angry that she beat upon Mark's great breast with her tiny fists. "It's not true! It's not true!" she cried. "You know...."

Abruptly, Mark took fire. She was swept in his arms, clipped there, half-lifted from the deck to meet his lips that dipped to hers. She was like nothing in his grasp; she could not stir.... And from his lips, and circling arms, and great body the hot fire of the man flung through her.... She fought him.... But even in that terrific moment she knew that Joel had never swept or whelmed her so....

She twisted her face away.... And thus, from the shadow where they stood, she saw Joel. He was at the top of the cabin companion, looking toward them, his face illumined by the light from below. And she watched for an instant, frozen with terror, expecting him to leap toward them and plunge at Mark and buffet him....

Joel stood for an instant, unstirring. Then he turned, very quietly, and went down stairs again into the cabin....

She thought, sickly, that he had shirked; he had seen, and held his hand....

What was it Mark had said? Afraid....

Mark had not seen Joel. He kissed her again. Then she twisted away from him, and fled below.

Joel was at his desk. He did not look up at her coming; and she stood for an instant, behind him, watching his bent head....

Then she slipped into her own cabin, and snapped the latch, and plunged her face in her pillow to stifle bursting sobs.

XII

The *Nathan Ross* changed course that day; and the word went around the ship. It passed from man to man. There was whispering; and there were dark looks, flung toward Joel.

Joel kept the deck all day, silent, and watchful, and waiting. Mark spoke to him once or twice, asking what he meant to do. Joel told him nothing. He had fought out his fight the night before; he knew himself....

Mark and Finch talked together, during the morning. Joel watched them without comment. Later he saw Mark speak to the other mates, one by one. At dinner in the cabin, the mates were silent. Their eyes had something of shame in them, and something of venomous hate.... They already hated Joel, whom they planned to wrong....

The day was fair, and the wind drove them smoothly. There was no work to be done, never a spout on the sea. Joel, watching once or twice the whispering groups of idle men, wished a whale might be sighted; and once he sent Morrell and Varde to find tasks for the men to do, and kept them at it through the long afternoon, scraping, scrubbing, painting....

Priss kept to her cabin. When she did not appear at breakfast, Joel went to her door and knocked. She called to him: "I've a headache. I'm going to rest." He ordered that food be sent to her....

He stayed on deck till late, that night; but with the coming of night the ship had grown quiet, and most of the men were below in the fo'c's'le. So at last Joel left the deck to Varde, and went below. He sat down at his desk and wrote up the day's log....

Priss came to him there. She had been in bed; and she wore a heavy dressing gown over her night garments. Her hair was braided, hanging across her shoulders.

She sat down beside the desk, and when Joel could fight back the misery in his eyes, he looked toward her and asked:

"Is your head--better?"

She said very quietly: "Joel, I want to ask you something."

He wanted her sympathy so terribly, and her tone was so cool and so aloof that he winced; but he said: "Very well?"

"Mark says he asked you to take the ***Nathan Ross*** to get--the pearls he left on that island. Is that true?"

"Yes," said Joel.

"He says you would not do it."

"I will not do it," Joel told her.

"He says," said Priss quietly, "that you are afraid. He says that was your own word ... when he accused you. Is that true?"

If there had been any sympathy or understanding in her voice or in her eyes, he would have told her ... told her that it was for his ship and not for himself that he was afraid. But there was not. She was so cold and hard.... He would not seek to justify himself to her....

"Yes," he said quietly. "I used that word."

She turned her eyes quickly away from his, that he might not see the pain in hers.... She rose to go back to her cabin....

As she reached the door, some one knocked on the door that led to the main cabin; and without waiting for word from Joel, that door opened. Mark stood there. He came in, with Finch, and Varde, and old Hooper and young Morrell on his heels.... Priss shrank back into her cabin, closed the door to a crack, listened....

Joel got to his feet. "What is it?" he asked.

Mark bowed low, faced his brother with a cold and triumphant smile. "These gentlemen have asked me," he explained, "to tell you that we have decided to go fetch the pearls."

XIII

When Priss, through the crack in the door, heard what Mark had said, she shut the door of her cabin soundlessly, and crouched against it, listening. She was trembling....

There was a long moment when no one of the men in the after cabin spoke. Then big Jim Finch said suavely: "That is to say, if Captain Shore does not object."

Joel asked then: "What if I do object?"

Mark laughed. "If you do object, why--we'll just go anyway. But you'll have no share."

And surly Varde added: "We'd as soon you did object."

Mark bade him be quiet. "That's not true, Joel," he said. "You know, I wanted you in this, from the first. Your coming in will--prevent complications. With you in, the whole matter is very simple, and safe.... But without you, we will be forced to take measures that may be--reprehensible."

Joel did not speak; and Priss, trembling against the door, thought bitterly: "He's afraid.... He said, himself, that he is afraid...."

Dick Morrell begged eagerly: "Please, Captain Shore. There's a fortune for all of us. Mr. Worthen would tell you to do it...."

Joel said then: "I told Mark Shore in the beginning that I would not risk my ship. The enterprise is not lawful. The pearls were stolen in the beginning; murder hung around them. Bad luck would follow them--and there are blacks on the island to prevent our finding them, in any case."

"There's no harm in going to see," Morrell urged.

"'Tis far out of our proper way. Wasted time. And--the men should be thinking of oil, not of pearls."

Mark laughed. "That may be," he agreed. "But the men's thoughts are already on the pearls. They've no mind for whaling, Joel. They've no mind for it."

"I'm doubtful that what you say is true."

His brother snapped angrily: "Do you call me liar?"

"No," said Joel gently. "You were never one to lie, Mark." And Priss, listening, winced at the thing that was like apology in his tone. She heard Mark laugh again, aloud; and she heard the fat chuckle of Jim Finch. Then Mark said:

"It's well you remember that. So.... Will you go with us; or do we go without you?"

There was a long moment of silence before Joel answered. At last he said: "You're making to spill blood on the *Nathan Ross*, Mark. I've no mind for that. I'll not have it--if I can stop it. So ... I'll consider this matter, to-night, and give you your answer in the morning."

"You'll answer now," Varde said sullenly. "There's too much words and words.... You'll answer now."

"I'll answer in the morning," Joel repeated, as though he had not heard Varde. "In the morning. And--for now--I'll bid you good night, gentlemen."

Mark chuckled. "There's one matter, Joel. You've two rifles and a pair of revolvers in the lockfast by your cabin there. I'll take them--to avoid that blood-spilling you mention."

Priss held her breath, listening.... But Joel said readily: "Yes. Here is the key, Mark. And--I hold you responsible for the weapons."

Her anger at Joel for his submission beat in her ears; and she heard the jingle of the keys, and the scrape and ring of the weapons as Mark took them. He called to Joel as he did so: "They'll not leave my hands. Till the morning, Joel, my boy...."

The keys jingled again. Mark said: "We'll ask you to stay in the after cabin here till morning. And--Varde will be in the main cabin to see that you do it."

"I'll stay here," Joel promised.

"Then--we'll bid you good night!"

Priss heard Joel echo the words, in even tones. Then the door closed behind the men.... There was no further sound in the after cabin.

She opened her door. Joel stood by his desk, head drooping, one hand resting on the open log before him. She went toward him, and when he turned and saw her, she stopped, and studied him, her eyes searching his. And at last she said, so softly it was as though she spoke to herself:

"'All the brothers were valiant,' Joel. Are you--just a coward?"

He would not justify himself to her; he could only remember the shadowed deck beneath the boat house--Priscilla in his brother's arms.... He lifted his right hand a little, said sternly:

"Go back to your place."

She flung her eyes away from him, stood for an instant, then went to her cabin with feet that lagged and stumbled.

XIV

Joel lay for an hour, planning what he should do. He could not yield.... He could not yield, even though he might wish to do so; for the yielding would forfeit forever all control over these men, or any others. He could not yield....

Yet he did not wish to fight; for the battle would be hopeless, with only death at the end for him, and it would ruin the men and lose the ship.... Blood marks a ship with a mark that cannot be washed away. And Joel loved his ship; and he loved his men with something of the love of a father for children. Children they were. He knew them. Simple, easily led, easily swept by some adventurous vision....

He slept, at last, dreamlessly; and in the morning, when they came to him, he told them what he wished to do.

"Call the men aft," he said. "I'll speak to them. We'll see what their will is."

Mark mocked him. "Ask the men, is it?" he exclaimed. "Let them vote, you'll be saying. Are you master of the ship, man; or just first selectman, that you'd call a town meeting on the high seas?"

"I'll talk with the men," said Joel stubbornly.

Varde strode forward angrily. "You'll talk with us," he said. "Yes or no. Now. What is it?"

They were in the main cabin. Joel looked at Varde steadily for an instant; then he said: "I'm going on deck. You'll come...."

Priss, in the door of the after cabin, a frightened and trembling little figure, called to him: "Joel. Joel. Don't...."

He said, without turning: "Stay in your cabin, Priscilla." And then he passed between Varde and Finch, at the foot of the companion, and turned his back upon them and went steadily up the steep, ladder-like stair. Varde made a convulsive movement to seize his arm; but Mark touched the man, held him with his eyes, whispered something....

They had left old Hooper on deck. He and Aaron Burnham were standing in the after house when Joel saw them. Joel said to the third mate: "Mr. Hooper, tell the men to lay aft."

Mark had come up at Joel's heels; and Hooper looked past Joel to Mark for confirmation. And Mark smiled mirthlessly, and approved. "Yes, Mr. Hooper, call the men," he said. "We're to hold a town meeting."

Old Hooper's slow brain could not follow such maneuvering; nevertheless, he bellowed a command. And the harpooners from the steerage, and the men from forecastle and fore deck came stumbling and crowding aft. The men stopped amidships; and Joel went toward them a little ways, until he was under the boat house. The mates stood about him, the harpooners a little to one side; and Mark leaned on the rail at the other side of the deck, watching, smiling.... The revolvers were in his belt; the rifles leaned against the after rail. He polished the butt of one of the revolvers while he watched and smiled....

Joel said, without preamble: "Men, the mates tell me that you've heard of my brother's pearls."

The men looked at one another, and at the mates. They were a jumbled lot, riff-raff of all the seas, Cape Verders, Islanders, a Cockney or two, a Frenchman, two or three Norsemen, and a backbone of New England stock. They looked at one another, and at the mates, with stupid, questioning eyes; and one or two of them nodded in a puzzled way, and the Cape Verders grinned with embarrassment. A New Englander drawled:

"Aye, sir. We've heard th' tale."

Joel nodded. "When my brother came aboard at Tubuai," he said quietly, "he proposed that we go to this island.... I do not know its position--"

Mark drawled from across the deck: "You know as much as any man aboard--myself excepted, Joel. It's my own secret, mind."

"He proposed that we go to this island," Joel pursued, "and that he and I go ashore and get the pearls and say nothing about them."

Varde, at Joel's side, swung his head and looked bleakly at Mark Shore; and one or two of the men murmured. Joel said quickly: "Don't misunderstand. I'm not blaming him for that. You must not. The pearls are his. He has a right to them...."

"What I want you to know is that I refused to go with him and get them on half shares. I could have had half, and refused....

"Now he has spread the story among you. And the mates say that I must go with you all, and get the things."

He stopped, and the eyes of the men were on him; and one or two nodded, and a voice here and there exclaimed in approval. Joel waited until they were quiet again; then he said: "These--pearls--have cost life. At least five men and a woman died in the getting of them. If we had them aboard here, more of us would die; for none would be content with his share....

"It's in my mind that they'd bring blood aboard the *Nathan Ross*. And I have no wish for that. But first--

"How many of you are for going after them?"

There was a murmur of assent from many throats; and Joel looked from man to man. "Most of you, at least," he said. "Is there any man against going?"

There may have been, but no man spoke; and over Joel's face passed a weary little shadow of pain. For a long moment he stood in the sun, studying them; and they saw his lips were white. Then he said quietly:

"You shall not go. The *Nathan Ross* goes on about her proper matters. The pearls stay where they are."

He shifted his weight, looked quickly toward his brother.... He was poised for battle. By the very force of his word, there was a chance he might prevail. He watched the men, in whose hands the answer lay. If he could hold them....

Hands clamped his arms, and Mark smiled across the deck. Finch and old Hooper on one side, Varde and Morrell on the other. And after the first wrench of his surprise, he knew it was hopeless to struggle, and stood quietly. Mark strolled across the deck, smiling coldly.

"If you'll not go, Joel, you must be taken," he said. And to the mates: "Bring back his arms."

Joel felt the cord slipped through his elbows and drawn tight and looped and made secure. Old Aaron Burnham pushed forward and tugged at them; and Joel heard him say: "They'll hold him fast, Captain Shore. Like a trussed fowl, sir. That he is...."

"Captain Shore?" That would be Mark, come into command of the ship again.

And Aaron added: "I've set the bolt on his cabin door, sir. Not five minutes gone."

Mark laughed. "Good enough, Aaron. You and Varde take him down. Varde, you'll stay in the after cabin. If he tries to get free, summon me. And--treat Mrs. Shore with the utmost courtesy."

Varde was at Joel's side; and Joel saw the twist of his smile at Mark's last word. For a moment, thought of Priss left Joel sick. He thrust the thought aside....

They took him down into the main cabin; Varde ahead, then Joel, and old Aaron close behind, his hand on Joel's elbow. Priss met them in the after cabin, crouching in a corner, white and still, her hands at her throat. Her eyes met his for an instant, before Varde led him toward his own cabin. Aaron, behind, looked toward Priss; and the girl whispered hoarsely:

"Is he--hurt?"

"He is not," said Aaron grimly. "We were most gentle with the man; and he made no struggle at all...."

Varde thrust Joel into the little cabin where his bunk was; and Joel heard the snick of a new-set bolt on the outer side of the door. He was alone, bound fast....

Before he left the deck, he had heard Mark cry an order to the man at the wheel. The telltale in the after cabin ceiling told him the **Nathan Ross** had changed her course again ... for Mark's island.... In the face of men, he had held himself steady and calm.... But now, alone in his cabin, he strained at his bonds, lips cracking over set teeth. He strained and tugged.... Hopeless....

No! Not hopeless! He felt them yield a little, a little more.... Then, with a tiny snap of sound, the coils were loose, and he shook the cords down over his wrists and hands. He caught them as they fell across his fingers, lest the sound of their fall might warn Varde, in the cabin outside his door; and--he was still stupefied by the surprise of this deliverance--he lifted the broken bonds and examined them....

A single strand had yielded, loosing all the rest. And where it had broken, Joel saw, it had been sliced all but through, with a keen blade.

Who? His thoughts raced back over the brief minutes of his bondage. Who?

No other but Aaron Burnham could have had the chance and the good will. Old Aaron.... And Aaron's knives were always razor sharp. Drawn once across the tight-stretched cord....

Aaron had freed him. Aaron....

He remembered something else. Aaron's words to Mark on deck. "I've set the bolt on his cabin door...."

Aaron had set the new bolt that was the only bar between him and the after cabin, where Varde stood watch. Aaron had set the bolt; and Aaron had cut his bonds. Therefore--the bolt must be flimsy, easily forced away. That would be Aaron's plan. A single thrust would open the way....

He turned toward the door; then caught himself, drew back, dropped on the bunk and lay there, planning what he must do.

XV

The discovery of Aaron's loyalty had been immensely heartening to Joel. If Aaron were loyal, there might be others.... Must be.... Not all men are false....

He wondered who they would be; he went over the men, one by one, from mate to humblest foremast hand. Finch and Varde were surely against him. Old Hooper--he and Aaron were cronies, and the other mates had left Hooper somewhat out of their movements thus far. Old Hooper might be, give him his chance, on Joel's side....

Old Hooper, and Aaron. Two. Dick Morrell? A boy, hot with the wonder and glamor of Mark's tale. Easily swung to either side. Joel thought he would not swing too desperately to the lawless side. But--he could not be counted on. What others were there?

Joel had brought his own harpooner from the **Martin Wilkes**. A big Island black. A decent man.... A chance. Besides him, there were three men who had served Asa Worthen long among the foremast hands. Uncertain quantities. Chances everywhere....

But--he must strike quickly. There was no time to sound them out. When his dinner was brought at noon, his broken bonds would be discovered. They would be more careful thereafter. Three hours lay before him....

He set himself to listen with all his ears; to guess at what was going on above decks, and so choose his moment. He must wait as long as it was safe to wait; he must wait till men's bloods ran less hot after the crisis of the morning. He must wait till sober second thought was upon them....

But there was always the chance to fear that Mark might come down. He could not wait too long....

He could hear feet moving on the deck above his head. The **Nathan Ross** had run into rougher weather with her change of course; the wind was stiffening, and now and then a whisk of spray came aboard. He heard Jim Finch's bellowing commands.... Heard Mark's laughter. Mark and Jim were astern, fairly over his head.

There were men in the main cabin. The scrape of their feet, the murmur of their voices came to him. Dick Morrell and old Hooper, perhaps....

It was through these men that Joel's moment came. Finch, on deck, shouted down to them.... Mark had decided to shorten sail, ease the strain on the old masts. Joel heard Morrell and Hooper go up to the deck....

That would mean most of the men aloft.... The decks would be fairly clear. His chance....

He wished he could know where Varde sat; but he could not be sure of that, and he could not wait to guess by listening. He caught up a blanket from his bunk, held it open in his hands, drew back--and threw himself against the cabin door.

It opened so easily that he overbalanced, all but fell. The screws had been set in punch holes so large that the threads scarce took hold at all. Joel stumbled out--saw Varde on the cushioned bench which ran across the stern. The mate was reading, a book from Joel's narrow shelf. At sight of Joel, he was for an instant paralyzed with surprise....

That instant was long enough for Joel. He swept the blanket down upon the man, smothering his cries with fold on fold; and he grappled Varde, and crushed him, and beat at his head with his fists until the mate's spasmodic struggles slackened. Priss had heard the sounds of combat, swept out of her cabin, bent above them. He looked up and saw her; and he said quietly:

"Get back into your place."

She cried pitifully: "I want to help. Please...."

He shook his head. "This is my task. Quick."

She fled....

He lifted Varde and carried him back to the cabin where he himself had been captive; and there, with the cords that had bound his own arms, he bound Varde, wrist and ankle; and he stripped away the blanket, and stuffed into Varde's mouth a heavy, woolen sock, and tied it there with a handkerchief.... Varde's eyes flickered open at the last; and Joel said to him:

"I must leave you here for the present. You will do well to lie quietly."

He left the man lying on the floor, and went out into the after cabin and salvaged the bolt and screws that had been sent flying by his thrust. He put the bolt back in place, pushed the screws into the holes, bolted the door.... No trace remained of his escape....

Priss stood in her own door. Without looking at her, he opened the door into the main cabin. That apartment was empty, as he had expected. The companion stair led to the deck....

But he could not go up that way. Mark and Jim Finch were within reach of the top of the stair; he would be at a disadvantage, coming up to them from below. He must reach the deck before they saw him.

He crossed the cabin to a lockfast, and opened it, and took out the two pairs of heavy ship's irons that lay there. Spring handcuffs that locked without a key.... He put one pair in each pocket of his coat.

There was a seldom used door that opened from the main cabin into a passage which led in turn to the steerage where the harpooners slept. Joel stepped to this door, slipped the bolt, entered the passage, and closed the door behind him.

It was black dark, where he stood. The passage was unlighted; and the swinging lamp in the steerage did not send its rays this far. The ***Nathan Ross*** was heeling and bucking heavily in the cross seas, and Joel chose his footing carefully, and moved forward along the passage, his hands braced against the wall on either side. The way was short, scarce half a dozen feet; but he was long in covering the distance, and he paused frequently to listen. He had no wish to encounter the harpooners in their narrow quarters....

He heard, at last, the muffled sound of a snore; and so covered the last inches of his way more quickly. When he was able to look into the place, he saw that two of the men were in their bunks, apparently asleep. The black whom he had brought from the ***Nathan Ross*** was not there. Joel was glad to think he was on deck; glad to hope for the chance of his help....

With steps so slow he seemed like a shadow in the semi-darkness, he crossed to the foot of the ladder that led to the deck. The men in their bunks still slept. He began to climb.... The ship was rolling heavily, so that he was forced to grip the ladder tightly.... One of the sleepers stirred, and Joel froze where he stood, and watched, and waited for endless seconds till the man became quiet once more.

He climbed till his head was on a level with the deck still hidden by the sides of the scuttle at the top of the ladder. And there he poised himself; for the last steps to the deck must be made in a single rush, so quickly that interference would be impossible....

He made them; one ... three.... He stood upon the deck, looked aft....

Mark and Jim Finch stood there, not ten feet away from him. Finch's back was turned, but Mark saw Joel instantly; and Joel, watching, saw Mark's mouth widen in a broad and mischievously delighted smile.

XVI

At the moment when Joel reached the deck, the other men aboard the *Nathan Ross* were widely scattered.

Varde, the second mate, he had left tied and helpless in the cabin. Two of the four harpooners were below in their bunks, asleep. The greater part of one watch was likewise below, in the fo'c's'le; and the rest of the crew, under Dick Morrell's eye, were shortening sail. In the after part of the ship there were only Mark Shore, Finch, a foremast hand at the wheel, old Aaron Burnham, and the cook. Of these, Mark, Jim, and the man at the wheel were in sight when Joel appeared; and only Mark had seen him.

Joel saw his brother smile, and stood for an instant, poised to meet an attack. None came. He swept his eyes forward and saw that he need fear no immediate interference from that direction; and so he went quietly toward the men astern. The broad back of Jim Finch was within six feet of him....

What moved Mark Shore in that moment, it is hard to say. It may have been the reckless spirit of the man, willing to wait and watch and see what Joel would do; or it may have been the distaste he must have felt for Jim Finch's slavish adulation; or it may have been an unadmitted admiration for Joel's courage....

At any rate, while Joel advanced, Mark stood still and smiled; and he gave Finch no warning, so that when Joel touched the mate's elbow, Finch whirled with a startled gasp of surprise and consternation, and in his first panic, tried to back away. Still Mark made no move. The man at the wheel uttered one exclamation, looked quickly at Mark for commands, and took his cue from his leader. Finch was left alone and unsupported to face Joel.

Joel did not pursue the retreating mate. He stepped to the rail, where the whaleboats hung, and called to Finch quietly:

"Mr. Finch, step here."

Finch had retreated until his shoulders were braced against the wall of the after house. He leaned there, hands outspread against the wall behind him, staring at Joel with goggling eyes. And Joel said again:

"Come here, Mr. Finch."

Joel's composure, and the determination and the confidence in his tone, frightened Finch. He clamored suddenly: "How did he get here, Captain Shore? Jump him. Tie him up--you--Aaron...."

He appealed to the man at the wheel, and to old Aaron, who had appeared in the doorway of the tiny compartment where his tools were stored. Neither stirred. Mark Shore, chuckling, stared at Finch and at Joel; and Finch cried:

"Captain Shore. Come on. Let's get him...."

Joel said for the third time: "Come here, Finch."

Finch held out a hand to Mark, appealingly. Mark shook his head. "This is your affair, Finch," he said. "Go get him, yourself. He's waiting for you. And--you're twice his size."

Give Finch his due. With even moral support behind him, he would have overwhelmed Joel in a single rush. Without that support, he would still have faced any reasonable attack. But there was something baffling about Joel's movements, his tones, the manner of his command, that stupefied Finch. He felt that he was groping in the dark. The mutiny must have collapsed.... It may have been only a snare to trap him.... He was alone--against Joel, and with none to support him....

Finch's courage was not of the solitary kind. He took one slow step toward Joel, and in that single step was surrender.

Joel stood still, but his eyes held the big man's; and he said curtly: "Quickly, Finch."

Finch took another lagging step, another....

Joel dropped his hand in his coat pocket and drew out a pair of irons. He tossed them toward Finch; and the mate shrank, and the irons struck him in the body and fell to the deck. He stared down at them, stared at Joel.

Joel said: "Pick them up. Snap one on your right wrist. Then put your arms around the davit, there, and snap the other...."

Finch shook his head in a bewildered way, as though trying to understand; and abruptly, a surge of honest anger swept him, and he stiffened, and wheeled to rush at Joel. But Joel made no move either to retreat or to meet the attack; and Finch, like a huge and baffled bear, slumped again, and slowly stooped, and gathered up the handcuffs....

With them in his hands, he looked again at Joel; and for a long moment their eyes battled. Then Joel stepped forward, touched Finch lightly on the arm, and guided him toward the rail. Finch was absolutely unresisting. The sap had gone out of him....

Joel drew the man's arms around the davit, and snapped the irons upon his wrist. Finch was fast there, out of whatever action there was to come. And Joel's lips tightened with relief. He stepped back....

He saw, then, that some of the crew had heard, and three or four of them were gathering amidships, near the try works. The two harpooners were there; and one of them was that black whom Joel had brought from the *Martin Wilkes*, and in whom he placed some faith. He eyed these men for a moment, wondering whether they were nerved to strike....

But they did not stir, they did not move toward him; and he guessed they were as stupefied as Finch by what had happened. So long as the men aft allowed him to go free, they would not interfere. They did not understand; and without understanding, they were helpless.

He turned his back on them, and looked toward Mark.

Mark Shore had watched Joel's encounter with Finch in frank enjoyment. Such incidents pleased him; they appealed to his love for the bold and daring facts of life.... He had smiled.

But now Joel saw that he had stepped back a little, perhaps by accident. He was behind the man at the wheel, behind the spot where Aaron Burnham stood. He was standing almost against the after rail, in the narrow corridor that runs fore and aft through the after house....

The pistols were in his belt, and the two rifles leaned on the rail at his side. Mark himself was standing at ease, his arms relaxed, his hands resting lightly on his hips and his feet apart. He swayed to the movement of the ship, balancing with the unconscious ease of long custom.

Joel went toward him, not slowly, yet without haste. He passed old Aaron with no word, passed the wheelman, and faced his brother. They were scarce two feet apart when he stopped; and there were no others near enough to hear, above the slashing of the seas and the whistle of the wind, his low words.

He said: "Mark, you've made a mistake. A bad mistake. In--starting this mutiny."

Mark smiled slowly. "That's a hard word, Joel. It's in my mind that if this is mutiny, it's a very peaceful model."

"Nevertheless, it is just that," said Joel. "It is that, and it is also a mistake. And--you are wise man enough to see this. There is still time to remedy the thing. It can be forgotten."

Mark chuckled. "If that is true, you've a most convenient memory, Joel."

Joel's cheeks flushed slowly, and he answered: "I am anxious to forget--whatever shames the House of Shore."

Mark threw back his head and laughed aloud. "Bless you, boy," he exclaimed. "'Tis no shame to you to have fallen victim to our numbers." But there was a heat in his tones that told Joel he was shaken. And Joel insisted steadily:

"It was not my own shame I feared."

"Mine, then?" Mark challenged.

"Aye," said Joel. "Yours."

Mark bent toward him with a mocking flare of anger in his eyes; and he said harshly: "You've spoken too much for a small man. Be silent. And go below."

Joel waited for an instant; then his shoulders stirred as though he chose a hard course, and he held out his hand and said quietly: "Give me the guns, Mark."

Mark stared at him; and he laughed aloud. "You're immense, boy," he applauded. "The cool nerve of you...." His eyes warmed with frank admiration. "Joel, hark to this," he cried, and jerked his head toward the captive Finch. "You've ripped the innards out of that mate of mine. I'll give you the job. You're mate of the *Nathan Ross* and I'm proud to have you...."

"I am captain of the *Nathan Ross*," said Joel. "And you are my brother, and a--mutineer. Give me the guns."

Mark threw up his hand angrily. "You'll not hear reason. Then--go below, and stay there. You...."

There are few men who can stand flat-footed and still hit a crushing blow;

but Joel did just this. When Mark began to speak, Joel's hands had been hanging limply at his sides. On Mark's last word, Joel's right hand whipped up as smoothly as a whip snaps; and it smacked on Mark's lean jaw with much the sound a whip makes. It struck just behind the point of the jaw, on the left hand side; and Mark's head jerked back, and his knees sagged, and he tottered weakly forward into Joel's very arms.

Joel's hands were at the other's belt, even as Mark fell. He brought out the revolvers, then let Mark slip down to the deck; and he stepped over the twitching body of his brother, and caught up the two rifles, and dropped them, with the revolvers, over the after rail.

Mark's splendid body had already begun to recover from the blow; he was struggling to sit up, and he saw what Joel did, and cried aloud: "Don't be a fool, boy. Keep them.... Hell!" For the weapons were gone. Joel turned, and looked down at him; and he said quietly:

"While I can help it, there'll be no blood shed on my ship."

Mark swept an arm toward the waist of the ship, and Joel looked and saw a growing knot of angry men there. "See them, do you?" Mark demanded. "They're drunk for blood. It's out of your hands, Joel. You've thrown your ace away. Now, boy--what will you do?"

The men began to surge aft, along the deck.

XVII

THE story of that battle upon the tumbling decks of the **Nathan Ross** was to be told and re-told at many a gam upon the whaling grounds. It was such a story as strong men love; a story of overwhelming odds, of epic combat, of splendid death where blood ran hot and strong....

There were a full score of men in the group that came aft toward Joel. And as they came, others, running from the fo'c's'le and dropping from the rigging, joined them. Every man was drunk with the vision of wealth that he had built upon Mark Shore's story. The thing had grown and grown in the telling; it had fattened on the greed native in the men; and it was a monstrous thing now, and one that would not be denied.... The men, as they moved aft, made grumbling sounds with their half-caught breath; and these sounds blended into a roaring growl like the growl of a beast.

To face these men stood Joel. For an instant, he was alone. Then, without word, old Aaron took his stand beside his captain. Aaron held gripped in both hands an adze. Its edge was sharp enough to slice hard wood like cheese.... And at Joel's other side, the cook. A round man, with greasy traces of his craft upon his countenance. He carried a heavy cleaver. There is an ancient feud between galley and fo'c's'le; and the men greeting the cook's coming with a hungry cry of delight....

Joel glanced at these new allies, and saw their weapons. He took the adze from Aaron, the cleaver from the other; and he turned and hurled them behind him, over the rail. And in the moment's silence that followed on this action, he called to the men:

"Go back to your places."

They growled at him; they were wordless, but they knew the thing they desired. The cook complained at Joel's elbow: "I could use that cleaver."

"I'll not have blood spilled," Joel told him. "If there's fighting, it will be with fists...."

And Mark touched Joel lightly on the shoulder, and took his place beside him. He was smiling, a twisted smile above the swollen lump upon his jaw. He said lightly: "If it's fists, Joel--I think I'm safest to fight beside you."

Joel looked up at him with a swift glance, and he brushed his hand across his eyes, and nodded. "I counted on that, Mark--in the last, long run," he said. Mark gripped his arm and pressed it; and in that moment the long, unspoken enmity between the brothers died forever. They faced the men....

One howled like a wolf: "He's done us. Done us in."

And another: "They're going to hog it. Them two...."

The little sea of scowling, twisting faces moved, it surged forward.... The men charged, more than a score, to overwhelm the four.

In the moment before, Joel had marked young Dick Morrell, at one side, twisted with indecision; and in the instant when the men moved, he called: "With us, Mr. Morrell."

It was command, not question; and the boy answered with a shout and a blow.... On the flank of the men, he swept toward them. And Joel's harpooner, and one of Asa Worthen's old men formed a triumvirate that fought there....

They were thus seven against a score. But they were seven good men. And the score were a mob....

It was fists, at the first, as Joel had sworn. The first, charging line broke upon them; and old Aaron was swept back, fighting like a cat, and crushed and bruised and left helpless in an instant. The fat cook dodged into his galley, and snatched a knife and held the door there, prodding the flanks of those who swirled past his stronghold. Joel dropped the first man who came to him; and likewise Mark. But another twined 'round Joel's legs, and he could not kick them free, and there was no time to stoop and tear the man away.

He and Mark kept back to back for a moment; but Mark was not a defensive fighter. He could not stand still and wait attack; and when his second man fell, he leaped the twisting body and charged into the clump of them. His black hair tossed, his eye was flaming; and his long arms worked like pistons and like flails. He became the center of a group that writhed and dissolved, and formed again. His head rose above them all.

The man who gripped Joel's legs, freed one hand and began to beat at Joel's body from below. Joel could not endure the blows; he bent, and took a rain of buffets on his head and shoulders while he caught the attacker by the throat, and lifted him up and flung him away. He staggered free, set his back against the galley wall; and when he shifted to avoid another attack, he found his place in the galley door. The fat cook crouched behind him, and Joel heard him shout: "I'll watch your legs, Cap'n. Give 'em the iron, sir. Give 'em th' iron."

Once Joel, looking down, saw the cook's knife play like a flame between his knees.... None would seek to pin him there.

The black harpooner fought his way across the deck to Joel's side. He left a trail of twisting bodies behind him. And he was grinning with a huge delight. "Now, sar, we'll do 'em, sar," he screamed. The sweat poured down his black cheeks; and his mouth was cut and bleeding. His shirt was torn away from one shoulder and arm....

"Good man," said Joel, between his panting blows. "Good man!"

Across the deck, one who had run forward for a handspike swept it down on young Dick Morrel's brown head. Morrell dodged, but the blow cracked his shoulder and swept him to the deck. The man who had fought beside him spraddled the prostrate body, and jerked an iron from the boat on the davits at his back and held it like a lance, to keep all men at a distance. A sheath knife sped, and twisted in the air, and struck him butt first above the eye, so that he fell limply and lay still....

Mark Shore had been forced against the rail near where Jim Finch was pinned. Big Finch was howling and weeping with fright; and a little man of the crew with a rat's mean soul who hated Finch had found his hour. He was leaping about the mate, lashing him mercilessly with a heavy end of rope; and Finch screamed and twisted beneath the blows.

So swiftly had the tumult of the battle arisen that all these things had come to pass before the harpooners asleep in the steerage could wake and reach the deck. When they climbed the ladder, and looked about them, they saw Morrell and his ally prostrate at one side, Joel and the cook holding the galley door against a half dozen men; and big Mark's towering head amidst a knot of half a dozen more. And one of the harpooners backed away toward the waist of the ship, watchful and wary, taking no part in the affair.

But the other ... He was a Cape Verder, black blood crossed with Spanish; and Mark Shore had tied him to a davit, once upon a time, and lashed him till he bled, for faults committed. He saw Mark now, and his eyes shone greedily.

This man crouched, and crossed to a boat--his own--and chose his own harpoon. He twisted off the wooden sheath that covered the point, and flung it across the deck; and he poised the heavy iron in his hands, and started slowly toward Mark, moving on tiptoe, lightly as a cat.

Mark saw him coming; and the big man shouted joyfully: "Why, Silva! Come, you...."

He flung aside the men encircling him. One among them held the handspike with which he had struck down Morrell; and Mark smote this man in the body, and when he doubled, wrenched the great club from his hands. He swung this, leaped to meet the harpooner.

They came together in mid-deck. The great handspike whistled through the air, and down. An egg-shell crunched beneath a heel.... Silva dropped.

Mark stood for an instant above him; and in that instant, every man saw the harpoon which Silva had driven home. Its heavy shaft hung, dragging on the deck; it hung from Mark's breast, high in the right shoulder; and the point stood out six inches behind his shoulder blade. It seemed to drag at him; he bent slowly beneath its weight, and drooped, and lay at last across the body of the man whose skull the handspike had crushed.

There were, at that moment, about a dozen of the men still on their feet; but in the instant of their paralyzed dismay, two things struck them; two furies ... Dick Morrell, tottering on unsteady feet, brandishing a razor-tipped lance full ten feet long. He came upon the men from the flank, shouting; and Joel, when he saw his brother fall, left his shelter in the galley door and swept upon them. The fat cook, with the knife, fought nobly at his side.

The men broke; they fled headlong, forward; and Joel and Morrell and the cook pursued them, through the waist, past the trypots, till they tumbled down the fo'c's'le scuttle and huddled in their bunks and howled....

A dozen limp bodies sprawled upon the deck, bodies of moaning men with heads that would ache and pound for days.... Joel left Morrell to guard the fo'c's'le, and went back among them, going swiftly from man to man....

Silva was dead. The others would not die--save only Mark. The iron had pierced his chest, had ripped a lung....

XVIII

He died that night, smiling to the last. He was able to speak, now and then, before the end; and Joel and Priss were near him, at his side, soothing him, listening....

He asked Joel, once: "Shall I tell you--where--pearls..."

Joel shook his head. "I do not want them," he said. "They have enough blood to turn them crimson. Let them lie."

And Mark smiled, and nodded faintly. "Right, boy. Let them lie...." And his eyes shone up at them; and he whispered presently: "That was--a fight to tell about, Joel...."

In those hours beside Mark, Priss completed the transition from girl to woman. She was very sober, and quiet; but she did not weep, and she answered Mark's smiles. And Mark, watching her, seemed to remember something, toward the last. Joel saw his eyes beckon; and he bent above his brother, and Mark whispered weakly:

"Treasure--Priss, Joel. She's--worth all.... Kissed her, but she fought me...."

Joel gripped his brother's hand. "I knew there was no--harm in you--or in her," he said. "Don't trouble, Mark...."

When old Aaron had stitched the canvas shroud, they laid Mark on the cutting stage; and Joel read over him from the Book, while the men stood silent by. Chastened men, heads bandaged, arms in slings ... Big Jim Finch at one side, shamed of face. Varde, sullen as ever, but with hopelessness writ large upon him. Morrell, and old Hooper....

Joel finished, and he closed the Book. "Unto the deep...." The cutting stage tilted, and the wave leaped and caught its burden and bore it softly down.... The sun was shining, the sea danced, the wind was warm on fair Priscilla's cheek....

And as though, the brief, dramatic chapter being ended, another must at once begin, the masthead man presently called down to Joel the long, droning hail:

"Ah-h-h-h! Blow-w-w-w-w!"

And he flung his arm toward where a misty spout sparkled in the sun a mile or two away. Minutes later, the boats took water; and the **Nathan Ross** was about her business again.

*   *   *   *   *

Joel wrote in the log that night, with Priscilla beside him, her fingers in his hair. Priscilla had been very humble, till Joel took her in his arms and comforted her....

He set down the ship's position; he recorded their capture, that day, of a great bull cachalot; and then:

"... This day Mark Shore was buried at sea. He died late last night, from wounds received when he fought valiantly to put down the mutiny of the crew. Fourth brother of the House of Shore...."

And below, the ancient and enduring epitaph:

"'All the brothers were valiant.'"

Priscilla, reading over his shoulder, pointed to this line and whispered sorrowfully: "But I--called you coward, Joel." He looked up at her, and smiled a little. "I know better now," she said. "So--give me the pen ... And close your eyes...."

He heard the scratch of steel on paper; and when he opened his eyes again he saw that Priscilla had underscored, with three deep strokes, the first word of that honorable line.

The Codes Of Hammurabi And Moses
W. W. Davies

QTY

The discovery of the Hammurabi Code is one of the greatest achievements of archaeology, and is of paramount interest, not only to the student of the Bible, but also to all those interested in ancient history...

Religion   **ISBN:** *1-59462-338-4*   **Pages:132**
MSRP $12.95

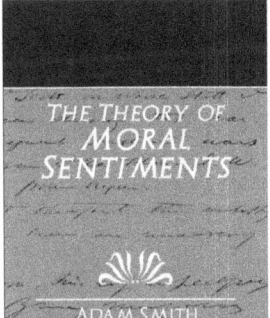

The Theory of Moral Sentiments
Adam Smith

QTY

This work from 1749. contains original theories of conscience amd moral judgment and it is the foundation for systemof morals.

Philosophy **ISBN:** *1-59462-777-0*   **Pages:536**
MSRP $19.95

Jessica's First Prayer
Hesba Stretton

QTY

In a screened and secluded corner of one of the many railway-bridges which span the streets of London there could be seen a few years ago, from five o'clock every morning until half past eight, a tidily set-out coffee-stall, consisting of a trestle and board, upon which stood two large tin cans, with a small fire of charcoal burning under each so as to keep the coffee boiling during the early hours of the morning when the work-people were thronging into the city on their way to their daily toil...

Pages:84

Childrens   **ISBN:** *1-59462-373-2*   *MSRP $9.95*

My Life and Work
Henry Ford

QTY

Henry Ford revolutionized the world with his implementation of mass production for the Model T automobile. Gain valuable business insight into his life and work with his own auto-biography... "We have only started on our development of our country we have not as yet, with all our talk of wonderful progress, done more than scratch the surface. The progress has been wonderful enough but..."

Pages:300

Biographies/   **ISBN:** *1-59462-198-5*   *MSRP $21.95*

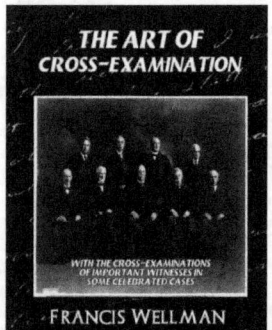

The Art of Cross-Examination
Francis Wellman

I presume it is the experience of every author, after his first book is published upon an important subject, to be almost overwhelmed with a wealth of ideas and illustrations which could readily have been included in his book, and which to his own mind, at least, seem to make a second edition inevitable. Such certainly was the case with me; and when the first edition had reached its sixth impression in five months, I rejoiced to learn that it seemed to my publishers that the book had met with a sufficiently favorable reception to justify a second and considerably enlarged edition. ..

Reference   **ISBN: *1-59462-647-2***

Pages:412

MSRP $19.95

On the Duty of Civil Disobedience
Henry David Thoreau

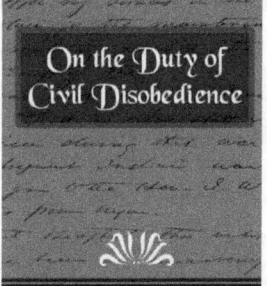

Thoreau wrote his famous essay, On the Duty of Civil Disobedience, as a protest against an unjust but popular war and the immoral but popular institution of slave-owning. He did more than write—he declined to pay his taxes, and was hauled off to gaol in consequence. Who can say how much this refusal of his hastened the end of the war and of slavery ?

Law   **ISBN: *1-59462-747-9***

Pages:48

MSRP $7.45

Dream Psychology Psychoanalysis for Beginners
Sigmund Freud

Sigmund Freud, born Sigismund Schlomo Freud (May 6, 1856 - September 23, 1939), was a Jewish-Austrian neurologist and psychiatrist who co-founded the psychoanalytic school of psychology. Freud is best known for his theories of the unconscious mind, especially involving the mechanism of repression; his redefinition of sexual desire as mobile and directed towards a wide variety of objects; and his therapeutic techniques, especially his understanding of transference in the therapeutic relationship and the presumed value of dreams as sources of insight into unconscious desires.

Psychology   **ISBN: *1-59462-905-6***

Pages:196

MSRP $15.45

The Miracle of Right Thought
Orison Swett Marden

Believe with all of your heart that you will do what you were made to do. When the mind has once formed the habit of holding cheerful, happy, prosperous pictures, it will not be easy to form the opposite habit. It does not matter how improbable or how far away this realization may see, or how dark the prospects may be, if we visualize them as best we can, as vividly as possible, hold tenaciously to them and vigorously struggle to attain them, they will gradually become actualized, realized in the life. But a desire, a longing without endeavor, a yearning abandoned or held indifferently will vanish without realization.

Pages:360

Self Help   **ISBN: *1-59462-644-8***

MSRP $25.45

www.bookjungle.com *email: sales@bookjungle.com fax: 630-214-0564 mail: Book Jungle PO Box 2226 Champaign, IL 61825*

QTY

The Rosicrucian Cosmo-Conception Mystic Christianity *by Max Heindel*   ISBN: *1-59462-188-8* **$38.95**
The Rosicrucian Cosmo-conception is not dogmatic, neither does it appeal to any other authority than the reason of the student. It is: not controversial, but is: sent forth in the, hope that it may help to clear...   New Age/Religion Pages 646

Abandonment To Divine Providence *by Jean-Pierre de Caussade*   ISBN: *1-59462-228-0* **$25.95**
"The Rev. Jean Pierre de Caussade was one of the most remarkable spiritual writers of the Society of Jesus in France in the 18th Century. His death took place at Toulouse in 1751. His works have gone through many editions and have been republished...   Inspirational/Religion Pages 400

Mental Chemistry *by Charles Haanel*   ISBN: *1-59462-192-6* **$23.95**
Mental Chemistry allows the change of material conditions by combining and appropriately utilizing the power of the mind. Much like applied chemistry creates something new and unique out of careful combinations of chemicals the mastery of mental chemistry...   New Age Pages 354

The Letters of Robert Browning and Elizabeth Barret Barrett 1845-1846 vol II   ISBN: *1-59462-193-4* **$35.95**
by Robert Browning and Elizabeth Barrett   Biographies Pages 596

Gleanings In Genesis (volume I) *by Arthur W. Pink*   ISBN: *1-59462-130-6* **$27.45**
Appropriately has Genesis been termed "the seed plot of the Bible" for in it we have, in germ form, almost all of the great doctrines which are afterwards fully developed in the books of Scripture which follow...   Religion/Inspirational Pages 420

The Master Key *by L. W. de Laurence*   ISBN: *1-59462-001-6* **$30.95**
In no branch of human knowledge has there been a more lively increase of the spirit of research during the past few years than in the study of Psychology, Concentration and Mental Discipline. The requests for authentic lessons in Thought Control, Mental Discipline and...   New Age/Business Pages 422

The Lesser Key Of Solomon Goetia *by L. W. de Laurence*   ISBN: *1-59462-092-X* **$9.95**
This translation of the first book of the "Lernegton" which is now for the first time made accessible to students of Talismanic Magic was done, after careful collation and edition, from numerous Ancient Manuscripts in Hebrew, Latin, and French...   New Age/Occult Pages 92

Rubaiyat Of Omar Khayyam *by Edward Fitzgerald*   ISBN: *1-59462-332-5* **$13.95**
Edward Fitzgerald, whom the world has already learned, in spite of his own efforts to remain within the shadow of anonymity, to look upon as one of the rarest poets of the century, was born at Bredfield, in Suffolk, on the 31st of March, 1809. He was the third son of John Purcell...   Music Pages 172

Ancient Law *by Henry Maine*   ISBN: *1-59462-128-4* **$29.95**
The chief object of the following pages is to indicate some of the earliest ideas of mankind, as they are reflected in Ancient Law, and to point out the relation of those ideas to modern thought.   Religion/History Pages 452

Far-Away Stories *by William J. Locke*   ISBN: *1-59462-129-2* **$19.45**
"Good wine needs no bush, but a collection of mixed vintages does. And this book is just such a collection. Some of the stories I do not want to remain buried for ever in the museum files of dead magazine-numbers an author's not unpardonable vanity..."   Fiction Pages 272

Life of David Crockett *by David Crockett*   ISBN: *1-59462-250-7* **$27.45**
"Colonel David Crockett was one of the most remarkable men of the times in which he lived. Born in humble life, but gifted with a strong will, an indomitable courage, and unremitting perseverance...   Biographies/New Age Pages 424

Lip-Reading *by Edward Nitchie*   ISBN: *1-59462-206-X* **$25.95**
Edward B. Nitchie, founder of the New York School for the Hard of Hearing, now the Nitchie School of Lip-Reading, Inc, wrote "LIP-READING Principles and Practice". The development and perfecting of this meritorious work on lip-reading was an undertaking...   How-to Pages 400

A Handbook of Suggestive Therapeutics, Applied Hypnotism, Psychic Science   ISBN: *1-59462-214-0* **$24.95**
by Henry Munro   Health/New Age/Health/Self-help Pages 376

A Doll's House: and Two Other Plays *by Henrik Ibsen*   ISBN: *1-59462-112-8* **$19.95**
Henrik Ibsen created this classic when in revolutionary 1848 Rome. Introducing some striking concepts in playwriting for the realist genre, this play has been studied the world over.   Fiction/Classics/Plays 308

The Light of Asia *by sir Edwin Arnold*   ISBN: *1-59462-204-3* **$13.95**
In this poetic masterpiece, Edwin Arnold describes the life and teachings of Buddha. The man who was to become known as Buddha to the world was born as Prince Gautama of India but he rejected the worldly riches and abandoned the reigns of power when...   Religion/History/Biographies Pages 170

The Complete Works of Guy de Maupassant *by Guy de Maupassant*   ISBN: *1-59462-157-8* **$16.95**
"For days and days, nights and nights, I had dreamed of that first kiss which was to consecrate our engagement, and I knew not on what spot I should put my lips..."   Fiction/Classics Pages 240

The Art of Cross-Examination *by Francis L. Wellman*   ISBN: *1-59462-309-0* **$26.95**
Written by a renowned trial lawyer, Wellman imparts his experience and uses case studies to explain how to use psychology to extract desired information through questioning.   How-to/Science/Reference Pages 408

Answered or Unanswered? *by Louisa Vaughan*   ISBN: *1-59462-248-5* **$10.95**
Miracles of Faith in China   Religion Pages 112

The Edinburgh Lectures on Mental Science (1909) *by Thomas*   ISBN: *1-59462-008-3* **$11.95**
This book contains the substance of a course of lectures recently given by the writer in the Queen Street Hail, Edinburgh. Its purpose is to indicate the Natural Principles governing the relation between Mental Action and Material Conditions...   New Age/Psychology Pages 148

Ayesha *by H. Rider Haggard*   ISBN: *1-59462-301-5* **$24.95**
Verily and indeed it is the unexpected that happens! Probably if there was one person upon the earth from whom the Editor of this, and of a certain previous history, did not expect to hear again...   Classics Pages 380

Ayala's Angel *by Anthony Trollope*   ISBN: *1-59462-352-X* **$29.95**
The two girls were both pretty, but Lucy who was twenty-one who supposed to be simple and comparatively unattractive, whereas Ayala was credited, as her Bombwhat romantic name might show, with poetic charm and a taste for romance. Ayala when her father died was nineteen...   Fiction Pages 484

The American Commonwealth *by James Bryce*   ISBN: *1-59462-286-8* **$34.45**
An interpretation of American democratic political theory. It examines political mechanics and society from the perspective of Scotsman James Bryce   Politics Pages 572

Stories of the Pilgrims *by Margaret P. Pumphrey*   ISBN: *1-59462-116-0* **$17.95**
This book explores pilgrims religious oppression in England as well as their escape to Holland and eventual crossing to America on the Mayflower, and their early days in New England...   History Pages 268

QTY

The Fasting Cure *by Sinclair Upton*　　　　　　　　　　　　ISBN: *1-59462-222-1*　**$13.95**
In the Cosmopolitan Magazine for May, 1910, and in the Contemporary Review (London) for April, 1910, I published an article dealing with my experiences in fasting. I have written a great many magazine articles, but never one which attracted so much attention... New Age/Self Help/Health Pages 164

Hebrew Astrology *by Sepharial*　　　　　　　　　　　　　ISBN: *1-59462-308-2*　**$13.45**
In these days of advanced thinking it is a matter of common observation that we have left many of the old landmarks behind and that we are now pressing forward to greater heights and to a wider horizon than that which represented the mind-content of our progenitors... Astrology Pages 144

Thought Vibration or The Law of Attraction in the Thought World　ISBN: *1-59462-127-6*　**$12.95**

by William Walker Atkinson　　　　　　　　　　　　　　　　　Psychology/Religion Pages 144

Optimism *by Helen Keller*　　　　　　　　　　　　　　　ISBN: *1-59462-108-X*　**$15.95**
Helen Keller was blind, deaf, and mute since 19 months old, yet famously learned how to overcome these handicaps, communicate with the world, and spread her lectures promoting optimism. An inspiring read for everyone... Biographies/Inspirational Pages 84

Sara Crewe *by Frances Burnett*　　　　　　　　　　　　　ISBN: *1-59462-360-0*　**$9.45**
In the first place, Miss Minchin lived in London. Her home was a large, dull, tall one, in a large, dull square, where all the houses were alike, and all the sparrows were alike, and where all the door-knockers made the same heavy sound... Childrens/Classic Pages 88

The Autobiography of Benjamin Franklin *by Benjamin Franklin*　ISBN: *1-59462-135-7*　**$24.95**
The Autobiography of Benjamin Franklin has probably been more extensively read than any other American historical work, and no other book of its kind has had such ups and downs of fortune. Franklin lived for many years in England, where he was agent... Biographies/History Pages 332

Name	
Email	
Telephone	
Address	
City, State ZIP	

☐ **Credit Card**　　　　　　☐ **Check / Money Order**

Credit Card Number	
Expiration Date	
Signature	

Please Mail to:　Book Jungle
　　　　　　　　PO Box 2226
　　　　　　　　Champaign, IL 61825
　or Fax to:　　　630-214-0564

ORDERING INFORMATION

web: *www.bookjungle.com*
email: *sales@bookjungle.com*
fax: *630-214-0564*
mail: *Book Jungle PO Box 2226 Champaign, IL 61825*
or PayPal *to sales@bookjungle.com*

Please contact us for bulk discounts

DIRECT-ORDER TERMS

**20% Discount if You Order
Two or More Books**
Free Domestic Shipping!
Accepted: Master Card, Visa,
Discover, American Express